Begin Again

Begin Again

A Stay Novella

By Jennifer Probst

1001 DARK NIGHTS
PRESS

Begin Again
A Stay Novella
By Jennifer Probst

1001 Dark Nights

Copyright 2020 Triple J Publishing Inc
ISBN: 978-1-970077-96-4

Foreword: Copyright 2014 M. J. Rose

Cover photo credit © Annie Ray/ Passion Pages

Published by 1001 Dark Nights Press, an imprint of Evil Eye Concepts,
Incorporated

Also From Jennifer Probst

The Stay Series
The Start of Something Good
A Brand New Ending
All Roads Lead to You

The Sunshine Sisters
Love on Beach Avenue
Temptation on Ocean Drive

The Billionaire Builders
Everywhere and Every Way
Any Time, Any Place
All or Nothing At All
Somehow, Some Way

Searching for Series:
Searching for Someday
Searching for Perfect
Searching for Beautiful
Searching for Always
Searching for You
Searching For Mine

The Marriage to a Billionaire series:
The Marriage Bargain
The Marriage Trap
The Marriage Mistake
The Marriage Merger
The Marriage Arrangement
The Books of Spells

Executive Seduction

All the Way

Sign up for the 1001 Dark Nights Newsletter
and be entered to win a Tiffany Key necklace.

There's a contest every month!

Go to www.1001DarkNights.com to subscribe.

**As a bonus, all subscribers can download
FIVE FREE exclusive books!**

Dedication

For all the employees and volunteers who work at animal rescue and welfare organizations. You believe all animals deserve to be safe and loved and back up your beliefs by action.

And for all the people fighting for animal rights – the belief that animals have the right to be free from exploitation, domination, and abuse by humans.

Thank you all for making a difference.

One Thousand and One Dark Nights

Once upon a time, in the future…

*I was a student fascinated with stories and learning.
I studied philosophy, poetry, history, the occult, and
the art and science of love and magic. I had a vast
library at my father's home and collected thousands
of volumes of fantastic tales.*

*I learned all about ancient races and bygone
times. About myths and legends and dreams of all
people through the millennium. And the more I read
the stronger my imagination grew until I discovered
that I was able to travel into the stories... to actually
become part of them.*

*I wish I could say that I listened to my teacher
and respected my gift, as I ought to have. If I had, I
would not be telling you this tale now.
But I was foolhardy and confused, showing off
with bravery.*

*One afternoon, curious about the myth of the
Arabian Nights, I traveled back to ancient Persia to
see for myself if it was true that every day Shahryar
(Persian: شهریار, "king") married a new virgin, and then
sent yesterday's wife to be beheaded. It was written
and I had read that by the time he met Scheherazade,
the vizier's daughter, he'd killed one thousand
women.*

*Something went wrong with my efforts. I arrived
in the midst of the story and somehow exchanged
places with Scheherazade — a phenomena that had
never occurred before and that still to this day, I
cannot explain.*

*Now I am trapped in that ancient past. I have
taken on Scheherazade's life and the only way I can
protect myself and stay alive is to do what she did to
protect herself and stay alive.*

*Every night the King calls for me and listens as I spin tales.
And when the evening ends and dawn breaks, I stop at a
point that leaves him breathless and yearning for more.
And so the King spares my life for one more day, so that
he might hear the rest of my dark tale.*

*As soon as I finish a story... I begin a new
one... like the one that you, dear reader, have before
you now.*

Chapter One

"We have an issue."

Chloe Lake glanced up from her buried desk and gave a sigh. Vivian was technically her boss, but they'd worked side-by-side the past year and emerged with both respect and a strong friendship. Of course, they had the same goal, but Chloe had observed a tangle of relationships in animal rescue organizations that were sometimes unhealthy. She'd learned a majority of people who fought for animal welfare didn't like humans, which was a bitch when dealing with politicians, lobbyists, PR companies, and the public.

Thank God, Chloe had learned young how to shine both in the spotlight and behind the scenes. It was probably why she'd risen up the ranks at Advocates for Animals and would soon take over Vivian's job when she left for a bigger position.

"We always have issues. If we were in a romantic relationship, we'd be in therapy," Chloe said.

Vivian grinned. Her trademark black pantsuit confirmed she'd been in meetings today. If she was with her animals, she wore jeans and a T-shirt. "Funny, Lake. But I'm not talking about us. I'm talking about this clusterfuck from the Spagarelli case. They dropped the suit."

Shock barreled through her. The hoarding case had been in the papers and their organization had stepped in to provide safe shelter for almost fifty dogs and cats hoarded and abandoned in a private home of horror. To Chloe, it'd been a tight case. "How?" she asked.

"Prosecutors are overloaded and they couldn't get enough for the judge to warrant a conviction. The real problem is the Spagarellis can turn around and just do it again."

Frustration and a simmering fury threatened, but her consistent practice of keeping her emotions stable helped ward off trouble. Vivian had no qualms about losing her temper, sometimes quite publicly, but it was part of her make-up and passion for the job. With her petite stature, waterfall of dark hair and gorgeous almond shaped eyes, she looked like a delicate piece of china ready to please.

Until she opened her mouth.

Vivian used her appearance like a weapon, taking her opponents off-guard with her ruthless focus, stubbornness, and raw honesty. Chloe had immediately experienced a girl crush the moment she stopped being intimidated.

Chloe tore off her black reading glasses and dropped them on the desk. Her thoughts whirled. "God, each time I think I've seen everything I'm schooled on my naivety. What's the plan?"

Vivian narrowed her gaze with a touch of ruthlessness. "Fight back, of course. We're bringing a civil suit against her. I've got a lawyer coming in to join us. He's been working with the Animal Defense Fund and has experience with neglect and hoarding cases. I want you to work with him specifically on this case. You're my point person. Get him up to speed and provide anything he wants—I want to move quickly on this. I also got some kickback from some of the shelters who can't take on anymore animals, so we need to circle back and place five more."

Chloe nodded, her mind already clicking through the endless tasks she needed to quickly finish or delegate. Working for an animal rescue organization full-time had always been her dream, and Advocates for Animals fulfilled a career goal. Ever since she began working for the Bishop horse rescue farm when she was nineteen, the need to help the voiceless animals had wormed its way in her blood. She'd been gifted to find her true path, but the deeper she got involved, she realized it was an emotionally draining, undercompensated, overworked career.

She still couldn't imagine doing anything else.

Chloe focused on the wins, not the losses. Just like her father had taught her.

They quickly discussed the mechanics of dispersing her current cases and brainstormed on some places that might take the last five dogs. "Keep me updated on any issues. I hope you didn't have a social life scheduled or anything."

"I've found fun overrated lately," she teased back, used to the time demands of the job.

"I find that hard to believe for the newly crowned Bachelorette of New York City."

Chloe rolled her eyes. "That was the worst thing to happen to me. The press hounds me enough, now I'm on the radar for every social media paparazzi, too." The popular online magazine, Females Today, was geared toward the twenty-something crowd and loved to create surveys and polls that quickly went viral. Unfortunately for her, the new issue featured not only her work, but her down-to-earth fashion, which boasted regular stores rather than high-priced designers. She wished the month would be over already, so the hype would finally die down and she could get a bit more privacy.

"I think you've been holding out on me." Her boss cocked her hip and regarded her with sly curiosity. That's when Chloe knew they'd downshifted to gossip. "You still dating that Chris Evans lookalike?"

She held her breath for a few precious seconds and hoped for the flock of butterfly wings. But as usual, her tummy was frustratingly silent. Pushing away the silly, adolescent thought, she nodded. "Yep. We're supposed to go to dinner this week."

Vivian whistled. "Any action yet? I'm imagining that man knows how to wield his shield…well."

Chloe laughed. "Think it's supposed to be a sword, but I like the imagery. God, no, we're not at that point. We're still getting to know each other."

Vivian wrinkled her nose. "Known him long enough to grab some action. You're way too mature for me, Lake. And cautious. Most hot single women who are the darling of the press would be taking advantage of some serious bed hopping. Are you worried about scandals?"

The question made her pause and think. Was she? She'd been in the spotlight since she was young, with a father who was once the NYC mayor, and now served as the current governor for the past two years. She'd struggled for a while in her early college years, acting out in spectacular fashion, resentful of being stuck under a microscope for her father's career, but now it was just part of her everyday life. In fact, she'd found her social media status quite useful in soliciting funds for Advocates for Animals and helping change the law. Networking and connections were both a blessing and curse and could be used for good or evil. Her father had taught her that lesson early, and to never take a favor without knowing what it would cost the soul.

"I don't think so," she said. "I just prefer going slow and getting to know a guy before I take him to bed. Drew seems amazing, but so did the last one. Learning he only wanted me to get to my father was a bit of a confidence killer."

Vivian shuddered. "Lake, you can't compare Drew to that slimy weasel. And if he'd known anything about your father, he would've realized the governor doesn't take lightly to his daughter getting played."

She couldn't help the laugh that escaped her lips at the memory. Dad had always been overprotective, especially after losing her mother so young. Even though Chloe was capable of fighting her own battles, she had to admit she got a bit of satisfaction after the weasel found himself frozen out from his high-society friends he'd been so proud of.

She might work for the greater good, but she still loved a worthy payback.

"True. How about you? Hot date this week?"

Vivian snorted. "Of course. He's cute, loves to cuddle, and adores me."

Chloe lifted a brow. "Rufus?"

"Correct. My pup is better than another crushing disappointment. If you find another Chris Evans, do me a favor. Throw him my way. I know exactly how to work his shield."

A laugh bubbled from her lips. She loved how Vivian worked hard and played harder. "Got it. When is the suit coming?" she asked.

Vivian glanced at her watch. "Tomorrow. Let's get our crap together so we can dive right in when he arrives."

"Pizza, tacos, or sushi?" she called out.

"Comfort food, Lake. Pizza all the way. With pepperoni."

Her boss disappeared down the hall. Chloe glanced at the lit-up phone lines, overloaded inbox, and endless piles of papers. Then she took a deep breath, trying to clear her mind so she could be her best for the fur babies who needed her. Most of the lawyers in animal welfare were good intentioned, smart individuals who took the job for the cause rather than the pay, but Chloe had come across many who seemed to own inflated egos and an entitled sense of power. Nothing pissed her off faster than a man who believed a law degree trumped all the other workers who tirelessly sacrificed their time.

She'd do everything in her power to stop another abuser in this world.

She hoped the suit held the same goal, because she'd be stuck with him for a while.

Pushing the thought aside, Chloe got back to work.

Chapter Two

Owen Salt paused outside the door, his hand clenching into a death-grip around his briefcase.

His life was about to change.

He took a few moments to calm his thundering heart and hoped he hadn't taken the ultimate gamble for nothing. All his hard work over the past few years to transform not only his career, but the man he was had been concentrated into a single goal.

Chloe Lake.

He squared his shoulders and knocked.

"Come in!"

This time, he didn't hesitate. He walked into her office, set his briefcase down, and waited for her to tear her glance from the computer.

His gaze swept over her cramped office, the finely organized chaos a staple of an overworked rescue agency, but it was the woman behind the desk who commanded his full attention.

Time stopped, then raced backwards until he was once again that awkward, young kid, staring at the most beautiful girl he'd ever seen. Even now, prepared for the shock of emotion that punched through him, he was struck a bit dumb and mute as he greedily took in her appearance.

Her hair was shorter now, barely touching her shoulders, a dark sable brown with deep hints of mahogany. He remembered running his fingers through the strands, the silky pull and dance of silk rising to meet him. Her face was turned toward her screen, red lips pursed as she silently read. A pair of trendy black glasses perched on her nose. He'd memorized every angle of her face until she haunted his dreams. Heart-shaped face.

Sharp, angular cheekbones, rounded chin, and a pert nose she'd always groaned about. He remembered kissing it while she fought to get away, her giggles rising to his ears like music. Remembered rolling in the green grass of the meadow, limbs entangled, lips pressed together, the haunting scent of sunshine and daisies permeating his senses and wrecking him for anyone after her.

His throat tightened but he remained still and stoic. Waiting.

She looked up.

The naked flash of vulnerability and searing pain almost made him stumble back. Shock flared in those cobalt blue depths, but he dove beyond the surface, desperate for the other emotions that he could build on; desperate for any type of hope.

There.

One precious, fleeting moment of longing flared pure and bright. And he knew he'd do everything in his power to exploit that lingering feeling because it meant she hadn't forgotten him.

She pushed back in her chair and stumbled to her feet, eyes wide in her face. "Owen? Wh—what are you doing here?"

He offered a small smile. "I'm back in New York. It's been a long time."

As if realizing she'd already shown him too much, a wall slammed down between them. She stiffened, her hands politely clasped in front of her like she faced a bored politician rather than the man who'd broken her heart. And he had. Badly. But if he was going to have a chance at redemption, he needed to focus on tiny steps. A flash of admiration tangled with disappointment as he watched her quickly compose herself and emanate a cool professionalism. Her voice was still husky, but tipped with ice. "I see. Well, to say this is a surprise is an understatement. Are you visiting your family?"

He nodded. "This weekend. Will stop by the Bishop farm, too, of course. Have you seen them lately?"

"Yes. Dad, Alyssa and I try to get out there regularly. They're all doing well. Mia and Ethan's daughter, Evie, will be turning one soon. Harper's expansion has been a success and she's able to rescue so many more horses."

He smiled, his heart full from the image of the beloved farm expanding with children and animals who took care of one another. The Bishops had changed his life, along with Chloe. He thought of them as his second family. "I stayed in touch," he said, not wanting her to think he'd abandoned them when he moved away.

Her lips pursed like she'd eaten something bad. "Glad you didn't leave everyone behind for something bigger and better," she said. Her light tone contradicted the hardness in her gaze.

He winced, regretting his last comment. She'd wanted to stay in touch, asked if they could be friends, but he couldn't. Chloe Lake wasn't a woman to be kept neatly sidelined. He'd known if it wasn't a clean break, he'd never be able to change into the man he'd needed to be. "I'm sorry, Chloe," he said, struggling to find the right words. "It's just that I—"

She waved a hand in the air, cutting him off. "No, don't. There's nothing left to apologize for, or explain. God knows, too many years have passed for us to trot back down memory lane." Her smile was stiff and her laugh forced. "I'm glad you stopped in, Owen. It was nice to see you and know you're doing well. But I have a ton of work to do so now's not a good time."

He cocked his head to study her. The black T-shirt pulled snugly across her breasts, the logo exclaiming *Be Part of the Solution, Not the Problem, Adopt Don't Shop!* Her short black skirt emphasized the flare of her hips and long, bare legs. Once, every sweet inch of her body had belonged to him. Standing across the room, her face closed to his probing stare, she was now a stranger.

He'd accept it. For now. Over the next few weeks, he'd have the opportunity to work with her on a cause they both believed in. He needed to use that small entryway to re-connect. "Okay. Should I introduce myself to the others? Or maybe you can direct me to my workspace while I'm here?"

She blinked. "What are you talking about?"

It took him a few beats to realize she didn't know. Was it possible no one told her who she'd be partnering with? He cleared his throat. "I'm the lawyer from the Animal Defense team. We're supposed to work together on the Spagarelli case."

Her jaw dropped. She quickly snapped it closed and shook her head. "No, that's not possible. You live in California."

"I used to. I finished my internship in LA, then joined Animal Defense. Got my law degree under their tutelage and was recently certified to practice in New York." He took in her slightly trembling hands as she lifted them to push back her bangs. Damnit, it wasn't supposed to happen like this. He'd figured she had enough time to anticipate his arrival, but now, it was like facing a wounded warrior who refused to admit weakness. His voice softened. "I thought you knew."

"The lawyer was supposed to arrive tomorrow."

"I figured I'd start early."

"Why are you taking on a case here? Why now?"

The truth spilled from his lips with ease. "It was time to come home."

She jerked, then lifted her chin. Defense lines carved into her face. "How convenient for you. My fault, I guess. I should have asked the suit's name."

The tinge of bitterness made him flinch. He looked down at his slightly rumpled charcoal suit and conservative tie. He'd never be into designer stuff, and was more comfortable in jeans and a T-shirt, but he'd embraced his new career and dressed the part. "Never thought I'd be dubbed a suit." He gave a lopsided smile, trying to lighten the mood. "Remember when Hei-Hei rushed me and I ended up falling into the mud pile? He clucked like a damn victory chant. Took me forever to get the stink out of my hair and skin." Memories of them together on the rescue farm, falling in love under the hot summer sun, horseback riding through the vibrant green meadows, laughing and caring for the animals together, hit him full force. His gut clenched with the need to get closer, inhale her scent, touch her smooth cheek. But he no longer had that right.

"I remember. But now you're a suit." Her blue eyes lit up like a lightning strike. "This case is important to us. I'll work with you to stop those SOBs from hurting any more animals. I'll be polite and respect the relationship we had. What I won't do is pretend we can ever go back or fall into some convenient friendship, talking about the good times we experienced. I just…can't." She turned on her heel and headed back to the safety of her desk. "You'll be working in here with me. I'll tell Jack to bring in your desk and you can set up in that corner. I need to finish up a few leftover projects first. I can be ready to attack this fresh tomorrow. Agreed?"

It was the tiny break in her voice that made him nod. This was hard for her. What she didn't realize was how much worse it was for him, because she didn't know he'd come back to New York for her.

For a second chance. A chance to love her the way he'd always imagined. As a man who'd made his own way and could finally give himself fully. But she wasn't ready to hear his explanations or excuses. Not yet.

"Understood."

"Vivian is down the hall, last room on the right. She'll get you anything you need."

With those final words, she sat back down, focused on her screen, and resumed typing.

Owen shut the door gently behind him.

For years, he'd wondered if he could still feel the same. Wondered if too much time had passed and too many changes occurred to experience the strong pull of rightness he'd always felt around her. The sense of knowing he'd found his soul mate, even at nineteen years old.

But looking into those deep blue eyes was like the first time all over again.

Nothing had changed. His heart still belonged to her.

Now he just had to prove he'd left for a loftier reason and that they were meant to be together.

It was a good thing he liked a challenge.

* * * *

The door clicked.

Chloe stopped typing and tangled her shaking fingers together.

Oh, God, he was back.

Not only in New York. Here. In her second home, the place she poured her heart and soul into. He'd be working in her space, physically close. Late nights. Sharing take-out. Trapped. It was like a nightmare unveiling in gruesome slow motion, and no way to wake up.

What was she going to do?

Jumping to her feet, she grabbed her hot pink stress ball from her desk, squeezing madly as she paced. Her mother had once told her there was no such thing as coincidence, and everything happened in the universe to lead people to their destiny. She'd always loved the theory, holding it close to her heart when things seemed hopeless.

Now? She wanted to scream for her mother to explain what the hell this could possibly mean. Had she done something wrong to deserve punishment? Was this payback for a deeper crime in her past? Or was the universe just a big jokester, like the Greek gods of mythology moving humans around for their humorous entertainment?

Chloe groaned and squeezed harder. The mushy texture had just enough give to satisfy her. Out of all the cases, in all the world, why did he have to push into hers? She briefly considered telling Vivian she wanted out, but the idea of quitting and allowing him to win pissed her off. After all, he'd left her. He'd been the one who calmly told her they shouldn't be friends and the break should be complete. He was the one who decided to show up in her office, talking about beloved memories, like everything was fine and they could easily become beer buddies.

Jerk. She fumed and paced, trying to follow the wild threads of her emotions. Had she been cool and calm enough? Had he glimpsed she'd wanted to fall to her knees in agony when she'd looked up to see him standing in front of her, broad shoulders framing the doorway, his thick, curly hair now tamed neatly back, dressed in a proper suit like a grown-up instead of a rebellious young guy who wanted to laugh, have fun, and tackle life as it came rather than make plans?

God, he'd changed. He seemed taller, more fit. Calm, as if he'd found his center and confidence over the years. He'd grown a goatee, the sexy scruff hugging his lush lips and framing his jaw. But it was his eyes that did her in. The palest summer sky blue. Always filled with laughter, a bit of mischief, and a naked admiration that made her feel like the most beautiful woman on the planet. She'd found his crush sweet at first. He was two years younger, a freshman in college, and she'd never imagined seeing him as more than a friend or little brother type. Until that fateful dance at a wedding that changed everything.

Chloe pushed the memory out of her head. He had no right to march in here with those baby blues and throw her world into chaos. His gaze practically drilled into her, probing, searching for the girl she used to be with him. Chloe refused to give him even a hint of that girl ever again. He wasn't allowed to demand anything from their past—he'd made his choice when she begged him, pride splintered helplessly around her, to stay. The scene still made her squirm with humiliation. Begging him to stay. Begging him to love her.

Hearing him say no. The resolute look on his face when he uttered the word, splintering her heart like a bullet. The way he'd never reached out, not even a drunken, lonely text to say he missed her and maybe he made a mistake. How many nights had she cried herself to sleep, cradling her aching chest to stop the pain?

Too many.

Slowly, she calmed. Chloe couldn't allow him to step back into her life and throw it into ruins. She had everything she'd worked for: a great job with meaning, emotional stability, a close relationship with her father, friends, and the possibility of love one day. Owen's presence hurt, but maybe it'd been the shock of seeing him when she wasn't prepared. Now her defenses would be up and instilled. She'd keep her focus on the case. Her life didn't have to change at all—this was just a small bump in the road. If she channeled her mother's beliefs, maybe he'd been sent to finally lock the door of her heart and allow her freedom.

Maybe it was time to truly put her first love behind her. For good.

She placed the stress ball back in its place. Owen was here for work, plain and simple. He'd help with the case and then move on. New York was a big city so even if he lived here, it should be easy enough to avoid him. She refused to allow him to make her uncomfortable when he was the one who'd left. Chloe would treat him with professional respect and remain politely distant so he didn't get any ideas. She'd channel all of her political training to keep herself safe, yet pleasant enough to do her job.

Satisfied with her empowering thoughts, she got back to work.

Chapter Three

Owen watched her from his corner. She was a master multi-tasker, able to juggle a phone call while typing out an email, the buzz of energy visible around her aura. He remembered when they first began dating. His idea of a great night was kicking back with some illegally fetched beers, watching a baseball game on TV or hanging with his friends in the dorm or woods. Things were simple because he'd taught himself not to want anything.

Until he wanted Chloe. There'd never been a girl who'd struck him mute the moment he looked into her eyes. Suddenly, he wanted to be worthy of her attention. He'd spent that first summer on the Bishop rescue horse farm following her around, hanging on each word while she taught him the inner workings of the farm. Her passion and love for the animals, for the structure, for the goal of rescuing the abused and helpless, stirred his inner soul. But no matter what he did, she never looked at him the way he craved.

Once his community service was done, he'd returned to a life that no longer satisfied him. His friends suddenly struck him as lazy and unmotivated, their goals nothing but partying and finding ways to cause trouble for their own amusement. He began pulling back, searching for his own identity and a replacement for Chloe. He wanted to feel good again. Important.

Needed.

He got his shit together that year, and when he saw her again at Mia and Ethan's wedding, she finally gave him a second glance. One slow dance had sparked a new connection—one more of equals—and he'd used that moment to build a foundation, intent on showing Chloe he could be a man worthy of her attention.

And he'd succeeded.

Owen would have bet everything she'd be the one to break his heart one day. He'd prepped for the event the whole time, because inside, he knew he wasn't enough for her. Not long term.

Instead, he'd ended up breaking her heart and having to live with the awful knowledge for four long years.

It was time to not only make amends, but get her to see why it was necessary to leave her.

"Owen, I have to go soon—did you get all the necessary vet records you asked for? Dr. Weathers said he'd be happy to meet with you again to be a witness."

He shook his head to clear his thoughts of the past. "Yes, thanks. I'll reach out."

"Any response yet on the temporary restraining order?"

"Not yet, but it may take a few weeks. The court's been backed up lately. I'm keeping a close eye on it. You look nice."

She jerked back, her gaze full of that wary suspicion that gutted him. Once her soul had been cracked open. Now she barely glanced at him, choosing to distance herself in every way possible. It had only been a few days working in her office, but he already knew how she planned to play the long game. She was focusing only on the work and shut down any effort at personal conversation. She grabbed every opportunity to leave the room, stand apart from him, or rely on email rather than dialogue. The brick wall between them seemed unscalable. He needed to begin chipping it away piece by piece if he'd ever have a chance to re-connect. "Thanks."

"Going to a fundraiser?" he asked, keeping his tone easy. He noted her sleek long skirt that hugged her curves, and the yellow cotton blouse that hugged her shoulders, leaving all that gorgeous olive skin bare. Her hair had been pinned up, a few dark strands caressing her cheeks, leaving her nape exposed. She'd always been tall at about five nine, but with strappy, high heeled sandals, she reached his height, her gaze level with his, as if she'd needed the extra confidence to face him.

"No." He waited, but she seemed done. As the governor's daughter, her social calendar was pretty booked, and the press loved to follow her around, speculating on her new love interest or charity. He'd come back just in time. The magazine dubbing her Bachelorette of NYC would bring out hordes of suitors, desperate to date her. It didn't hurt she was young, single, and gorgeous, with a vibrant personality that popped on camera.

It had been another reason he'd decided to flee. One day, maybe he'd be able to explain so she understood.

Owen nodded in the following silence that seemed to ripple with undercurrents of tension. "I see. Good talk."

She spun on her heel, blue eyes shooting sparks of temper. "I have a date, okay? Not that it's any of your business. In fact, unless it pertains to the case, I don't think we really need to chat."

He pretended the breath hadn't been knocked out of him. Of course she was seeing someone. He just hoped it wasn't serious yet. "Chloe, I'm going to be here for a while. Can't we make a truce? You have every damn right to be pissed at me. Do you think I just happily moved on with my life without thinking about you and what I did to us?" Frustration tinged his tone. "I hoped with a bit of time, we'd be able to talk. I want to explain some things."

Sadness flickered over her features. Automatically, he rose from the chair and stepped forward to take her in his arms, wanting to give comfort, then stopped. Her voice was a soft whisper of sound, a caress to his ears and skin, light as gossamer. "It's not about anger anymore. It's about you wanting to step back into my life when you no longer know who I am. It's about you thinking a good explanation can wipe away the pain, even if I don't have a right to question why you wanted to leave. Because I realized I don't have that right, Owen. You shouldn't have to apologize to me for going after your dreams, even if I wasn't one of them. I mean, look at you." She lifted her arms, a humorless laugh escaping her lips. "You're a lawyer for an important organization at only twenty-six. You made it. And I'm so damn proud." Her lower lip quivered, then she pulled herself to full height, a calm settling over her. "I just don't want to talk about the past, or rehash all the things that led us here. Did you ever see the movie *LaLa Land*?"

He blinked, then shook his head. "No."

"Let's just say they both made choices that put them on different paths. They may not have ended up together, but they were happy. It was just an alternate vision than what could have been. Like us."

"Well, I hate that ending," he said. "It sucks."

Genuine laughter flashed in those baby blues, then faded. "Yeah, but it's real. I'll agree to stop treating you like a leper, but I don't want to be friends. That's my truth, and I hope you respect it. I've got to go. Text me with any issues. I'll see you tomorrow."

She left to go meet another man.

And she didn't look back.

* * * *

Dinner was perfect.

Drew took her to Felice, an intimate Italian restaurant that was a favorite of hers and her father's. She knew the places to dine when she wanted to court the press, and the haunts when she craved a bit of privacy.

Drew kept their dialogue fun and easy through the first course, his All American looks easy on the gaze. Now that Vivian called up images of Chris Evans, Chloe realized her friend was right. With his clean-cut blonde hair, dreamy eyes, and chiseled figure, he was a man who was comfortable and confident around women. He owned a successful finance business and set up a foundation to give to various not-for-profits. She wondered if he'd ever been awkward when he was young, or unsure of his future. Or followed a girl around with his heart in his eyes, not caring if he got hurt because she was worth it.

Stop thinking about Owen.

Chloe reached for her wine glass and took a sip. It was an expensive, hearty red that blended with her eggplant dish, bringing out layers of blackberry and currant flavors. It had taken her a while to begin liking wine, but now she appreciated a good pour, finding it a solid subject to make a connection with strangers. It had served her well at many parties, able to smoothly transition into talking about her charity once a proper bond had formed.

Drew gave her an easy smile, his hand reaching across to tangle with hers. "I'm glad you were able to come out tonight," he said. "I always termed myself a workaholic until I met you."

She laughed and returned the pressure of his hand. His grip was solid, his hand practically dwarfing hers as if swallowing it whole. She reminded herself it was a feeling of safety rather than control. "Sorry, we got a new case to work on. Hoarding and abuse. The owner escaped prosecution so we're deep into the civil suit. Have to make sure those animals stay safe, and they don't find a new place and start over again."

His face turned sympathetic. "That's awful. I sped up your application for Advocates for Animals so hopefully a decision can be made sooner on the amount we can give."

Unease curled in her stomach. "Drew, I don't want to use our relationship for any unfair advantage. I told you that—I want a fair and equal shot at being one of your foundation picks."

He grinned, flashing shiny white teeth. "Don't worry, everything is above board. Now let's switch to more pleasant subjects. I think you need a break from all the drama in your world. How's your father?"

She shifted in her seat and tamped down the irritation at how easily he was able to disconnect from issues that were passionate for her. Still, he was a finance guy, and one who dedicated his money to many different causes. She couldn't expect him to share all of her views on animal rescue. "Good. He's been embroiled in words with the President again, but he knows how to smooth things over when needed. Alyssa helps balance him."

"That's what a good woman does. I consider my mother the reason for my success. She always supported me, knew how to push, and taught me the value of ethics in today's world."

"That's so nice," she murmured, liking the way he spoke of his mom. "What about your dad?"

He wrinkled his nose. "Not so much. They're divorced, but I take good care of her. Give her anything she needs. It's another reason I connected with you right away. Your close relationship with your dad showed me you have a real sense of family values. I need that in my life."

A strange foreboding trickled through her. Odd, it was a high compliment, but she felt as if she was being interviewed for being his prospective wife. She forced a laugh. "Well, I'm grateful we're good now, but we had some rocky times in the past. After losing my mom, it took me a while to find my way. I felt lost for a while, and he was so deep into his run for mayor, we fought a lot."

"But you realized your mistake and healed the rift. That's what families do. Forgive. Support each other without question. Isn't that what you want in your life, Chloe? A partner to share it all?"

She blinked, startled by the intensity in his blue-gray eyes. Drew's were like a misty storm. Owen's reminded her of a calm sky that stretched for miles, a safe place to drift, to dream, to be completely herself.

God, what was wrong with her?

"Sure. Down the road, I guess." She forced a smile. "I still have a lot I want to do before I make any long-term commitment."

He cocked his head, tapping his finger against his wine glass. "Of course. But I've always believed with the right person, you can achieve anything without sacrifice." He laughed, his eyes crinkling slightly at the corners. "Sorry, didn't mean to get so serious so quick. I'm known to be a bit intense at times."

She relaxed. "I can relate."

"Good. I wanted to see if you'd join me as my date for an upcoming business dinner. It'll be an intimate event, only a dozen people. I'm holding it at that new French restaurant getting all those rave reviews so it's still relatively formal."

"Oh, for the Foundation?"

"No, this one is for my investment corporation. But I promise it won't be filled with stuffy Wall Street executives. I have a nice mix of people I think you'd enjoy meeting. It's in two weeks. I can text you all the details."

She hesitated. She despised spending her precious nights at yet another formal affair, but she'd like to see Drew in his element and get to know more about him and his business. "Of course, I'd love to."

"Excellent. I'm assuming we're skipping dessert?"

She'd been looking forward to the tiramisu all night, but figured it would be awkward if she asked for it now. "I'll have a cappuccino," she said, hoping they gave her an extra biscotti with it.

"Me, too." He ordered, and the waiter cleared their table with quick efficiency. Drew's handsome face softened as he stared at her. "I don't want this to come off too strong, but I wanted you to know I've been thinking about you a lot." He shook his head, looking adorably self-conscious. "It's been a long time since I've been excited about a woman in my life. I just wanted you to know that."

Chloe waited for the excited leap in her chest from his declaration, but once again, her heart was disturbingly steady. But maybe that didn't matter? After all, she was twenty-eight years old, past the age of needing silly physical cues when her head said this man was a good fit for her. Other than a few chaste good-night kisses, they hadn't slipped into any type of intimacy.

She needed to kiss him tonight. Passionately. Raise the stakes. She refused to screw up an opportunity with a man just because she was stuck on a young boy from her past who didn't exist anymore.

"Thank you, Drew," she said, giving him a warm smile. "I'm excited about you, too."

They sipped their late-night coffee and fell into an easy dialogue. By the time he'd escorted her to his black Mercedes-Benz, Chloe was relaxed. They held hands as he deftly maneuvered through the crowded city streets and unbelievably, found an open parking space on her block. "Score," he murmured, and she laughed, already turning, her mind focused on him.

He cut the engine. Leaned in. Her hand drifted up to hesitantly touch his face, smooth and stubble free, his square cut jaw straight, full lips, and cut cheekbones straight from a superhero comic. "You're very handsome," she whispered.

He chuckled. "Thank you. But you are a work of art." He stroked her hair. "And it's officially our fifth date. Would you invite me up?"

Tension stiffened her muscles. She wasn't ready to sleep with him yet. There was something sacred about inviting a man into her bed. When she was young and reckless, she'd made a bunch of bad choices, sleeping with bad boys to prove nothing could hurt her, and it only made a bigger mess in her head. Now she accepted her need to go slow and refused to apologize for it. "I don't think tonight is a good idea," she said.

He nodded, taking the rejection with his normal ease. "Got it. Then I'll just have to show you how you make me feel right here."

He lowered his head and kissed her.

Chloe responded immediately, allowing her mouth to soften under his, her hands gripping his broad shoulders. He smelled of expensive cologne, a musky, ocean scent that should have driven her crazy. He knew what he was doing, expertly applying the perfect amount of pressure, slowly sliding his tongue with subtle precision, allowing her to warm up. Her body responded like a fine-tuned machine and she sank into the kiss, deliberately shutting her mind down to enjoy the moment.

When he finally lifted his head, satisfaction gleamed in his eyes. "You are delicious," he muttered. "I can't wait to see you again."

"Me, too." She smiled and grabbed her purse. "I better go. Thanks for dinner."

"Thanks for saying yes."

Chloe climbed out of the car and walked to her apartment building. Nodding to Art, the doorman, she took the elevator up to the eighth floor and entered her sacred space. Kicking off her heels, she went straight to her living room, got comfortable, and took out her phone.

He answered on the second ring. "Sweetheart! It's so good to hear from you. What's up?"

The sound of her father's voice was everything good in the world, and she leaned her head back on the sofa, closing her eyes. Funny, for so many years, she hid everything from him, refusing to share any of her feelings. Now she looked forward to their talks, and though she had many close friends who'd be there anytime, she preferred going straight to her father. "Hi, Dad. Am I interrupting?"

"There's nothing I could be doing where I'd consider you an interruption. You sound funny."

She laughed but it turned into a half sob. "I had a date. With Drew Dinkle."

A whistle cut over the phone. "That's great! I've always liked Drew. He's got his priorities straight—family values, hard work, and charity. If I had a choice to set you up with anyone, I'd pick Drew. How'd it go?"

"Great. He took me to Felice's."

"Our favorite place. See, he's winning already. How long have you been seeing him?"

"This was our fifth date. Dad, can I ask you something?"

"Sure."

"Is it better to be ruled by your heart or your head?"

A pause settled over the line. His voice was wary. "Ugh, I guess it depends on what type of decision you're making. For example, if you had the opportunity to make big bucks at a job or work with the animals for much less, what would you do?"

"I'd pick the animals."

"Right. So that's choosing with your heart, not your head. I think that's a good thing. But many toxic relationships have occurred by using the heart rather than the old noggin. You can't use it as an excuse to follow bad behavior. Make sense?"

"Yes." Her father always explained things logically, in a way that made perfect sense. "You're saying there's no simple answer. Each situation is independent of a choice."

"Correct. Honey, what's wrong?"

She took a breath and told him the truth. "Owen came back."

There were a few beats of dead silence. Then a low whisper. "I'm going to kill him. Did he dare to contact you? Tell me where he is right now, I'll take care of everything."

"No! Dad, is Alyssa there? I need her with you before you freak on me."

A feminine voice floated in the background, and then the shuffle of noise crackled. "Chloe? I'm here. Your father is getting his stress ball."

She laughed. "Good idea. I don't want to upset him, I just needed to talk."

"Understood. Tell me what's happening."

Chloe almost wept with relief. Alyssa was a gift. As her father's long-term assistant, they'd had a rocky path to their own love story, but eventually, they both triumphed and had gotten married last year. Chloe loved her like a second mom and felt as if her own mother had sent Alyssa to both of them with her blessing.

"Owen returned to New York. He's a lawyer for the Animal Defense Fund, and he's been assigned to the Spagarelli case."

"The civil action suit? Wait—I thought Owen was in California?" Alyssa asked.

"He was, but now he's home to stay. Even worse? We have to work together for the next few weeks. Vivian put me in charge."

Alyssa gasped. "Oh, this is bad. How did you react? Have you both talked it out, or are you ignoring him?"

"I told him he needs to keep his distance because we're no longer friends. He acted like we'd go back to hanging out just because we share a past—do you believe it?"

She sighed. "Men."

"Put her on speaker!" her father shouted. "I need to hear."

"Only if you're calm and listen," Alyssa said. "Chloe doesn't need a mob boss ready to explode."

"Hell, I'm no mob boss. I'd do this hit personally."

Chloe choked out a laugh. "Dad, I can handle myself. He just surprised me. I wasn't ready for him to stroll into my life after so many years and announce we'll be working together in a tiny office space."

"Did you look good when he saw you?" Alyssa asked.

"Yes, I did."

"Excellent." Her stepmother's satisfaction was purely female, and Chloe loved her even more for it. "I bet he's steeped in regret."

Her father spoke up. "Honey, listen to me. Owen means nothing to you now. You're with Drew, who's a perfect match. Just keep it to business and concentrate on this new romance. You deserve to be happy."

The flicker of unease grew to monstrous proportions. "That's what I'm trying to do. It's just that, well, I kind of—" She broke off and tried again. "I don't know why, but I, I—"

"Still have feelings for Owen," Alyssa finished.

Chloe bit her lower lip. The shame of the admission made her want to cringe. "Yeah."

Her father's voice vibrated with authority. "I have a plan. I'll make some calls and get him off the case. I'll find the perfect replacement and then he'll go away."

She shook her head even though her father couldn't see her. "No way. This isn't your life, Dad, and I can't have you using your position to fix stuff."

"What good is being governor if I can't fix stuff?"

She tried not to laugh at his stubbornness. "Fix injustice, okay? Not my life. I'll handle this. I think acknowledging I haven't let go of the past is the first step in letting go. Maybe this time with Owen is what I needed to finally move on."

"With Drew," her father said. "I agree. You can handle this."

Alyssa sighed. "As much as your father has a bromance going on, please go slow, Chloe. Don't rush into anything because you're trying to run from your feelings for Owen. That won't help anyone."

"I won't. Thanks, guys. I better go, I just needed to talk."

"We love you," Alyssa said.

"Call day or night if you change your mind on anything. Like getting Owen fired. Or hurt."

"I will, Dad. Love you both."

She ended the call. The heaviness in her chest lightened. She'd needed to verbalize the doubts to someone who knew how badly she'd been hurt. Alyssa was right. Her evening with Drew made her realize she needed to face the past so she could put it behind her for good. Focusing only on work had been putting a Band-Aid on the problem.

It was time to talk to Owen.

If she could make peace and realize they were never meant to be together long-term, she'd be able to focus on Drew and give him the shot he deserved. She couldn't kiss him again while thinking of another man. And that man was really a ghost, a man who didn't exist anymore other than in her dreams and memories. She needed to flush him out and the only way was to face him head on.

Her decision made, she went to bed.

Chapter Four

A dozen blood-red roses sat on her desk, and all Owen could think of was what Chloe had done with the bastard who'd sent them.

His mind tortured with images that made him want to bleach his brain, he cursed under his breath and filled up his coffee mug for the dozenth time. It was almost eleven am and she still hadn't shown.

Owen had the bad luck to be near the door when the floral carrier stepped in with her sunny smile, calling out Chloe's name. He'd quickly signed, his fingers awkwardly grabbing the elaborate arrangement while her friends oohed and ahhed over who the mystery man could be. Owen had wanted to rush into a private room and rip open the card to know his name, but he managed to smile calmly and bring them into her office.

For the next hour, he brooded, stared at the roses, and drank coffee.

What was he going to do?

Her stubborn refusal to talk threw all his plans awry. Why hadn't he realized he'd hurt her so deeply she didn't want anything to do with him? In his head, he'd constructed this big redemption scene. He'd explain why he left, she'd understand, and they'd agree to try again. Sure, he knew she dated regularly—but he'd kept a close eye on her social media, engaged with consistent talks with the Bishops, and inquired with a few contacts in the animal advocacy world. Everyone always confirmed she wasn't involved in a serious relationship. He figured he had enough time, but once again, he'd screwed it all up.

Owen sat down at his desk, glanced at the endless piles of files scattered around, and drummed his fingers on the battered old wood. He needed a better plan. A way to force her to be in his company without work. He'd seen a ridiculous movie once, where the broken-up couple were locked in a room for twenty-four hours, unable to escape, and when they emerged, they were back together. And that other one, where they got stranded in a snowstorm and worked out their issues.

He had to stop watching those damn Hallmark movies. It was wrecking his reality.

Her scent hit him full force before she launched herself past him, muttering madly under her breath as if in an effort to keep all her thoughts organized. She dropped her bag and began typing with flashing fingers. "I had an early morning meet-up with my friend, Ava, from the Rescue Center, who told me she knows someone who confirmed the Spagarellis' neighbors tried to notify authorities of the abuse but the lead got kicked around and no one followed up. I'm sending you the contact info now—we need to call ASAP. I don't think they even interviewed this guy, did they?"

Excitement hit. A new witness could be critical, especially with a messed-up report that never got properly filed. His phone dinged and he checked his sources. "No, he's not even on this list. I'm on it. Great work."

"Thanks."

"You got roses."

She paused, as if just processing her surroundings. Slowly, she turned her head, studying the explosion of perfect, full, fragrant blooms. "Hmm, seems I did." She plucked the card from the envelope, read it, then tucked it into her desk drawer. He watched her face, probing for any type of emotion, especially happiness, but it was like she wore a mask.

He kept talking. "They're beautiful. You must've made a memorable impression last night."

She arched her brow, crossed her arms in front of her chest, and regarded him coolly. "Think so?"

He threw up his hands in mock surrender. "Didn't mean anything by it."

"Sure you didn't. It's nice to feel appreciated. *Remembered*."

He jerked back slightly, her last word a stinging slap. "You're right. God knows you deserve to be treated like a queen. I just wonder if he knows you well at all."

A scathing laugh filled his ears. "He knows me just fine. Enough to know how much I love flowers."

"Yeah, but not roses." Her gaze narrowed but he rushed on. "You love wildflowers. A bunch of loud, bright colors in different shapes that never seemed to match. But when you put them together, they became extraordinary, like broken pieces suddenly whole." He smiled. "You mixed them with weeds, but refused to term them that. You said they were proof of how raw beauty is better than any hothouse flower that looks perfect but dies too soon. Remember?"

He waited for her to toss a biting retort and leave. Instead, a haunted expression flickered over her face, as if he'd suddenly broken through a wall. "Yeah. I remember."

A deep ache of wanting spread through him. His gaze locked on hers, and he dove deep, looking for the woman he knew and loved, urging her to give him a sign it wasn't too late. "Do you also remember when I stopped the car on our way to Minnewaska? I spotted that field filled with so many yellow and purple flowers it looked like a painting. I pulled over, raced up the hill, and picked you that bouquet."

"You got stung by a bee."

Owen laughed, shaking his head. "I did. Hurt like a mother. But your smile when I handed you those flowers filled me up for days on end. Sometimes, I still fall asleep at night remembering your smile and the way you made me feel I could take on the world because you loved me."

Her eyes widened, and she spun away, as if desperately needing space. "Don't."

"Sorry. I don't mean to upset you." A few beats of silence settled between them. "It was probably stupid anyway. Can you imagine receiving a bunch of daisies with the grass still hanging from the roots? I should have given you what you always deserved—roses, stargazer lilies, something beautiful and elegant and timeless." Emotion choked him, but he kept his voice neutral. "This guy at least sees that in you."

He prepared for the steely silence he probably deserved and tried to focus on the work. At least he could do this. Right a wrong. Save an animal. Make a small difference. It seemed to be the only thing left that soothed his soul and gave him purpose since her.

"Owen?"

"Yeah?"

"I hate roses. They're full of pretense." He held his breath, afraid to break the fragile connection, sensing something critical was about to be revealed. She still didn't look at him, but her voice had softened. "I took some daisies from that bouquet you gave me that day and kept them. Pressed them into my favorite book."

"*The Art of Racing in the Rain?*"

Her body shuddered. "Yes."

Owen couldn't take it anymore. He got up and walked over to her, standing a few inches behind. Buzzing waves of energy shot from her figure, but she kept her head down, refusing to face him. "Chloe, I'm begging you for one thing. Have dinner with me. Just once. Let me say what I need, even if you don't think I deserve it. There's so much that happened between us, the idea of you believing certain things is tearing me up inside."

"Do you really think a talk can change anything?" she finally asked.

"Yes, I do." He had to. It was the only thing to cling to, the powerful idea he could explain his heart and gain her forgiveness. The fantasy of his second chance drove him forward. "Please give me one night of your attention. If you still feel the same, I'll back off and won't bother you again."

Slowly, she turned to face him. Her features revealed a reluctant resolution that caused a twist of pain and elation. "Okay. Dinner. Tomorrow?"

He nodded. "I'll pick a quiet place, off the grid."

"Fine. Just one last thing."

"What?"

Her gaze drilled into his. "We may have very different intentions for this night, Owen. You need to accept it probably won't turn out the way you want."

He reached out to automatically touch her, froze, then dropped his hand. "Big risks for big rewards," he finally said. "You taught me that early on." At her puzzled look, he prodded her memory. "The protest at the meat packing plant. I told you it wouldn't change anything because I was afraid you might get hurt."

She nodded. "That's right, I remember. They threatened the protestors with violence, and it blew up in the media. But nothing happened. The plant never closed. We didn't go to jail. Why would you remember it?"

"Because it was the first time someone showed me to fight for what you believe in, even if you don't win. Especially if you don't win. My grandfather kept trying to explain the concept for years, but I waved it off as some random philosophy that made no sense. At the protest, the lesson suddenly sparked like a lightbulb moment." She cocked her head, listening intently. "All those years as a judge taught him it was about showing up every day with the intention to do good. To create justice in a small way. Many times he failed, but instead of believing he made no difference, he'd reset the next day and start anew."

His beloved grandfather had been tough, wise, and a constant presence in Owen's upbringing. Judge Bennett had been the one to sentence Chloe to community service at the Bishop farm, which changed her life. And when Owen had screwed up, he'd been given the same punishment. He'd hated every moment until Chloe came and changed his outlook—and his life. Losing him before being able to show him how Owen had changed was haunting, but he'd struggled to make peace and trust his grandfather knew.

"You drove that lesson home for me, Chloe. Because you showed up consistently at that plant, with your sign and your voice, even when most everyone else had left it behind and moved on to other cases. Now, it's shut down."

A ghost of a smile touched her lips. "Not from me yelling at workers behind the fence for months," she said.

"Maybe. Maybe not. You kept the protest relevant. You changed me. I just wanted you to know that."

He backed off and returned to his desk, giving her space. After a few minutes, he heard the click of her keyboard. Owen re-focused on his work, reminding himself the animals at the Spagarellis' deserved his full attention.

They worked together for the next few hours in complete harmony, with the scent of roses drifting in the air.

Chapter Five

Chloe looked around the dark, almost empty pub and paused. "Umm, is the food here okay?"

He laughed, lifting his hand to the lone bartender, who called out a greeting and motioned for Owen to take a seat. He picked an oversized, high-backed booth toward the back. "Yes. Giving you food poisoning on our first date would be an epic fail."

"It's not a date," she said automatically.

"Sorry. I meant evening out. It's nothing fancy, but I figured you'd be craving a decent burger. The pub caters mostly to the after-dinner crowd here—their bar menu and beer options are legendary."

There were so many restaurants in New York City she'd be able to spend the rest of her life dining at a new place every night and never get through them all. She appreciated all the sleek dark wood, matching bar stools, and impressive bar that displayed endless bottles of liquor, wine, and beer taps. She liked that he'd picked a casual place with no frills or impressive French food with tiny portions. "I don't eat meat," she said, glancing down at the menu.

"I know. I meant their veggie burgers—they make them to order. I'd also suggest the sweet potato fries. Or I can get onion rings and we can share."

Her lip quirked. Owen had always loved sharing. He had a deep appreciation for simple yet plentiful food. She remembered how they'd hang for hours together on the rooftop of Bacchus in New Paltz, the twinkling white lights creating their own world, even as the noisy crowds from the packed streets rose up and echoed through the air. "Are you a vegetarian, too?" she asked. He'd admired her but always said there hadn't been a steak he hadn't loved.

"Yep. Working with farm rescues and observing the practices of slaughterhouses turned me off eating animals."

"I understand. The more knowledge I gain, the less I seem to eat. Except pasta. Carbs seem to be my best friend and worst enemy."

He grinned, his gaze raking over her figure with male admiration. "You always looked amazing. Especially tonight."

Her brow arched. "I'm in jeans."

He gave a boyish shrug. "It was always my favorite outfit on you."

Pleasure coursed through her. Chloe had made sure to dress informal. No need to give him false pretenses she was here for anything other than closure. But staring at him now, she remembered how much she adored the way his gaze lit up whenever he laid eyes on her, making her feel like a goddess morning, noon, and night. It wasn't about clothes, or makeup, or being sexy for him. He'd been the first man to look past her surface and see all the junk hidden inside, stuff she'd never let anyone spot, always too embarrassed she was too needy, or weak, or boring. It had been the reason she'd dressed for attention years ago, fueling all that self-anger out into the world.

Mia and Ethan and the Bishop farm had changed everything for her.

And Owen. Always Owen.

The waitress came over and they quickly put in their orders. She returned with one Hefeweizen in the grapefruit flavor she loved, and a shot of whiskey for Owen. Chloe took a hearty sip, trying to calm her racing pulse.

God, he looked good. Like her, he was dressed in jeans but paired it with a bright blue button-down shirt. The color deepened his pale blue eyes. The material stretched across his impressive chest and clung to his broad shoulders. He'd filled out these past years, obviously adding in strength training to lose the lean skinniness he used to sport. The sexy goatee added a roughness to his features, a masculinity that made her stomach flip, then drop.

Damn. She was still attracted to him, but in a way, time had only made it worse. She ached to reach out and touch him, feel the roughness of his skin, test the hardness of muscle, slide her lips across his to see if they were as soft as she remembered.

"Yes."

Yanked back to reality, she tried hard not to blush. "Yes what?"

His gaze suddenly burned into hers. "Yes to everything you were thinking."

A hot ache settled between her thighs. This man who looked at her with an edge exuded a confidence that had never been there before. As if he'd figured out who he was and no longer needed to apologize or change to suit another. She wondered if he would kiss the same way: sweet, worshipful, deep. Wondered if the same spark would ignite, or if it would be just a physical connection without the emotional.

No. She needed to stop wondering and get some hard answers.

"You don't get to know what I'm thinking any longer," she said lightly, wrangling in the loose tendrils of heat whipping around them. "You wanted the opportunity to explain things. That's why I'm here."

He nodded, the intense glint in his eyes fading. "You're right. There are certain things you have to know."

Silence fell between them, pulsing with an awkward undertone as she watched him try to gather his thoughts to explain the breakdown of their relationship. Chloe cleared her throat, not ready to dive in. "I'm curious how you got here. How did your internship go in California?"

He visibly relaxed, shooting her a grateful glance. "Animal Welfare was a huge turning point. I'd only experienced some local community rescues here, so being in LA was like an eye opener. There were things happening that I'll never be able to unsee. I started out helping with the volunteers and assisting the full-timers, but I hadn't really found what segment I really wanted to dig into. Until I got assigned to help out the legal team on a specific abuse case. That changed everything."

Chloe recognized the visible emotion in his eyes, the way his fingers gripped the neck of the bottle when certain memories hit. Watching the cruelty of humans challenged the core of who she was—the frustration and rage of seeing helpless animals consistently hurt pushed her to compartmentalize the worst of it. The work was a delicate balancing act of caring enough not to be numb, but not getting lost in the rage where results could falter. Owen had worked with her at some shelters, but he'd never experienced a case from the front lines. "You never forget your first," she murmured.

"Exactly. I knew I didn't want to focus on fundraising, marketing, or get stuck in endless board meetings, trying to make nice with political or community members. But when I watched how concrete laws could make a difference, and how short-handed welfare law is because it's not the money maker, I knew I'd found my niche."

The waitress dropped off their burger platters with a cheerful smile, re-filled their waters, and glided away. Chloe smothered hers with ketchup and hot sauce and dug in.

Owen laughed. "Why am I not surprised you still ruin all your food with that stuff?"

She finished her first bite and rolled her eyes. "Hot sauce makes the world a better place. Do you still eat your stuff boring and plain? Or did your travels educate you on the finer details of dining?"

He carefully took off his lettuce, tomato, and onion, replaced the top bun, and lifted it up. "I want to taste the burger, not the junk on it. Plain rules."

It was a ridiculous argument they'd always had, and she felt a silly smile tug at her lips. "I refuse to engage in such a useless discussion. Keep going. You found law."

"I found law. This road, unfortunately, demanded a huge commitment—both financial and education. The good news is Animal Welfare saw my potential and worked to assign me a legal apprenticeship in lieu of law school with their partners, The Animal Defense Fund. My grandfather had left me a trust that helped pay my way so I could concentrate on my studies full-time. He still believed in me, even though I'd never shown him any proof."

His eyes glinted with grief, and she fought the urge to take his hand in hers. "I'm not surprised he believed in you, Owen. You made mistakes, and you were supposed to—you were only a freshman in college. He was a judge and focused his life on second chances. I wish you wouldn't be so hard on yourself."

He blew out a breath. "You're right. Hard to break the habit of blaming yourself sometimes. It's so damn easy."

She smiled, thinking of her own regrets regarding her choices. "Truth."

"Anyway, I studied and worked my ass off and passed the bar exam. Began taking on my own cases, but I soon realized my heart had never truly been in California. It was a place I needed to go to grow up and find my career. But I always knew I wanted to come home."

Her skin prickled with goose bumps. He said the words with a purpose and intention that clearly implied she was part of his goal. The question burst out of her mouth, demanding he verbalize what burned in his gaze. "Why? What was here for you, Owen?"

He uttered the word with a stark simplicity. "You."

Chloe dropped the rest of her burger on the plate, quickly wiping her fingers. "You don't get to come home to what you already rejected." Bitterness coated her tongue. "You don't get to rewrite the past because you suddenly romanticized what we were."

"You're right. But even when I left, I knew you had already claimed my heart. I knew I'd only be able to give other women pieces of it because I planned to come back to you as a changed man. A man who could stand as your full partner, not chase you around like a lost puppy, eventually being outgrown because I didn't know who I really was."

Her gaze narrowed. "I never looked at you like that. You did. And you did it so you'd have a good excuse to leave like a martyr, spouting a bunch of bullshit to yourself that it was for the future of us. Well, let me give it to you straight." She jabbed her finger in the air. "You destroyed us when I begged you to stay, and you left without a word. Like I was some sort of sacrifice you had to butcher for the greater good. God, I felt so stupid afterward. I gave you all I had, but it wasn't enough."

"You were always enough for me. I just wasn't enough for myself." He lifted his hands in the air with a tinge of desperation. "I didn't know how else to let go. Chloe, I was nineteen when I fell in love with you. When I graduated, I knew you'd changed me, but I had no idea how to become my own man. I felt as if I was continuously chasing after you in order to be enough, and eventually, you'd hate what I'd become. Even your father saw it clearly, as I bumbled around trying to decide how I could best support you, be with you, love you. But I had nothing for myself. I was nothing without you, and the realization scared the shit out of me."

She thought back to those idyllic times when she'd believed everything was perfect. Within their relationship, she'd found not only bliss, but a deep satisfaction that confirmed Owen was the one. She hadn't been prepared to meet him so young, but she'd remembered her mother's late-night whispers about her father, and how once they met, her heart had always belonged to him. Like Fate. Destiny. Soul mates rediscovering each other. Chloe had been willing to embrace and accept the magic, she'd always assumed Owen felt the same.

Looking back, had he ever felt as confident about their future? Had he felt trapped? Yes, he was two years younger. Yes, he'd been less settled than an older man who knew his career and path. To her, it was exciting to launch the discovery together—she'd never meant to overshadow.

Obviously, she'd been wrong about everything.

"I can't believe I'm processing the excuse, 'It was never you, it was me,'" she said.

He winced. "It's the truth. I was searching for an answer. When my grandfather's friend Jim reached out and asked if I'd be interested in coming to LA to intern with Animal Welfare, it seemed like the answer I'd been searching for. He was on the Board, so he could get me the position."

"I remember when you told me," she murmured. The memory of that awful night, when he explained he wanted to leave permanently for California, was etched in her vision. "I wanted to try and make it work long distance. You never gave us a chance."

"Because I needed to be on my own to figure out who I really was." His jaw clenched, and within his eyes, she glimpsed a flash of shame. "I needed to leave you in order to find myself."

The brutal words attacked her like stinging knives. "Yet you never thought to share this with me? You figured the best way to accomplish your task was to break up with me, give me no real explanations, and make me think it was something I lacked the entire time?"

"I was stupid. Scared. I was ashamed I couldn't be the man you thought I was, so it was easier to hide my reasons and escape. If only you knew how much I missed you. Four long years and I never stopped thinking of you. I always planned to come back."

She choked out a laugh. "Right. And what if I'd decided to marry someone else during that time stretch while you were finding yourself? Did you actually believe I was putting my life on hold for you, Owen?"

He shook his head. "It was a huge risk. I kept tabs on you constantly. Social media, the press, the Bishops, and some friends I'd kept in contact with. But I can't say I wouldn't have dropped it all and come back if there was someone you were serious about."

It was too much. She'd tried to make peace with the fallout, and now he was back, blowing it all back up. A part of her heard and understood his words. As horrible as his actions were, if he'd truly believed he was trying to find himself in order to come back to her, maybe there was a chance of forgiveness.

But she knew for a fact he was a liar.

Chloe stayed silent as the waitress cleared their plates and brought them two coffees. "And now you've decided it's time to stake your claim on me?"

He jerked back slightly, but his voice remained calm. "No. I decided I couldn't stand being away from you any longer. I kept watch on all the cases in New York, and when Advocates for Animals put out a call for legal help, I immediately requested to transfer. I always intended to come home, but this seemed like a sign."

"So after this case, no matter what happens, you're staying?"

"Yes. I'll be working in the central Animal Defense Fund office, helping organizations with their legal battles. I'm done running."

His declaration shot chills through her body. She sipped her coffee, seeking a different type of warmth. "I see. And you still attest you broke up with me because you wanted to become your own person? It had nothing to do with other women? Craving to play the field before you settle down? Be honest with me."

"No, Chloe. There was no one but you. I haven't been with another woman. That's the truth."

The breath was knocked out of her lungs from his statement. Wild hope surged, but she slammed it back down, refusing to be taken in again by declarations that were untrue.

"I saw you with that girl," she finally said, meeting his gaze head on. "On your Facebook page. She was half naked and all over you. So please don't lie and pretend there was no one else. I saw the post two weeks after you left, and you certainly weren't grieving. In fact, you'd refused to answer any of my desperate texts. Clearly, you'd moved on, and it wasn't just about a job."

Regret carved out the features of his face. The buried pain rose up again, but she choked it back. She refused to let him spin the past in a way that made him look misunderstood. Chloe sat in the chair, took another sip of coffee, and regarded him with a calm that belied her racing heart.

"There was no girl, Chloe," he said. "I put her up there on purpose because I knew you'd see it."

She jerked back, her fingers trembling around the mug. "You really are a bastard."

"You don't understand. You never did. I loved you too much. It took all the strength I had to leave you, and once I was in California, stuck in the life I thought would be the best, I was miserable. I got all of your texts, and I responded a million times, deleting each one. I knew if we spoke at all, I'd scrap it all and return to New York. To you. So I did the only thing to guarantee you wouldn't reach out to me again. I went to a party, had a few drinks, and took that selfie with a girl."

A humorless laugh ripped from his lips. "I didn't even know her name. But the moment I posted it, I knew I'd shut the door for good. I got home from that party and stayed in bed for two days straight, not able to leave the house. And then I got my ass up and got to work, because damned if I was going to lose you without making it worth it."

Her brain sifted through his words to find the real meaning, but it was like sludge through a filter. "Why, Owen? Why would you hurt me on purpose? Don't you know I would have supported anything you wanted to do? God, you make it sound like I wanted you as my damn boy toy rather than a partner. I knew there were things you dreamed of too! Why couldn't you have let me be part of it?"

"Because I never thought I was worthy of you."

The admission tore the breath from her lungs. She stared at the man across from her, the one who'd held her heart and soul with gentle hands and a sweet smile. Familiar blue eyes gleamed with too many emotions and memories, and the past and present tangled up together, blurring the boundaries. He'd changed, grown into a man with his own plans, exhibiting a confidence that had never been there before. Yet her heart recognized the seeds of the man she'd fallen in love with. "Why would you ever say that? Think that? Did I ever give you a reason to believe I was better than you?"

He shook his head, his hair catching the light and turning it to spun gold. "God, no. You made me feel the opposite, but it wasn't about you. Don't you remember how it was? I'd graduated from college with a half-assed degree I wasn't even going to use. You were already setting the world on fire. You got hired by the law firm, graduated with a business degree, and were making real changes with animal rescues." His gaze sparked with intensity. "You exhibited a fire and passion I'd never experienced before. You believed you could change the world, and I knew you could. Yet here I was, tagging behind you, trying to pretend I knew what I was doing."

Her jaw dropped. Why was he twisting the past to suit his vision? "You were just as involved! You worked at the Bishop farm, signed up for an internship at Pets Alive, and decided to go back to school for your master's."

"Sure, because I still had no idea what I wanted to do with my life." He leaned in, frustration flickering from his figure. "Because that's what you suggested I do."

"Are you blaming me for your insecurities?"

"No, not even close. I'm trying to explain how it was. I was twenty-two and had spent half my college days fucking around. My grandfather had been the only one left to believe I'd make my mark one day, and I lost him. I never showed him proof I'd ever succeed. My father left long ago, and it's not a damn excuse, but I struggled to figure out if it'd been something I did to make him leave."

"You never told me you felt like that," she murmured, flashing back to those brief instances she'd asked about his dad, and he'd shut down with a lopsided smile. He'd hidden that part of himself. The hurt that sliced through her was ridiculous. Yes, she'd told him everything, but maybe she'd been completely wrong about the relationship she believed they'd had.

"I wasn't even sure what I felt, babe." The familiar endearment scorched her ears, but she didn't tell him to stop. "Losing my grandfather messed me up a bit. I wanted to be so much better for him, for you, for myself. The only path that made sense was to give myself the time and space to grow into what I always wanted. A man to stand as your partner."

"You were always that to me. I just wish you would have told me this stuff instead of shutting down. Making me believe you didn't love me the way I loved you."

He'd never once confessed he felt intimidated by her. Suddenly, shame filled her, along with doubt. Was this what men thought of her? Was she so independent that she pushed everyone away, making them feel unworthy? Had she bullied him into leading a life she wanted instead of allowing him to choose? Had losing her mother so young twisted her into a woman who'd never be able to need a man the way they craved?

The thoughts spun in her head and sickened her stomach. Suddenly, she needed to get away and think. Process everything he'd thrown at her in the past hour. She jumped up from the booth and stumbled back a few steps. "I-I need a minute. I have to go."

A muscle clenched in his jaw. "Oh, hell, no. Not like this. Not believing what you're telling yourself right now." He threw down his napkin and stood up.

She shook her head, ready to scream. "Leave me alone." Vision blurred, she veered toward the back of the pub, down a shadowed hallway leading to the restrooms. The demons inside whispered, taunting, reaching deep into her insecurities and throwing them at her with a mad glee.

A firm grip on her arm stalled her escape. He turned her around and her back bumped up against the wall. Chloe tilted her head up to meet his gaze head on. "Everything you're thinking is wrong. It was my fault for the way I handled things. Never yours."

A shiver slid down her spine. He was mad. She rarely saw this side of him, his good-natured personality rarely allowing him to experience such volatile emotions, but the man a few inches in front of her was not the boy she remembered.

Pale blue eyes glinted with a fiery intent as he laid his fingers over her shoulders, holding her in place. The scent of him assaulted her full-force, a clean combination of lemon and soap, his breath scented with a sting of heated whiskey and coffee. There was no hesitation or searching for permission as his gaze raked over her with a simmering hunger that thrilled her to the core. She fought the feeling, hanging on to the mix of anger, frustration, and self-shame his words had evoked from within. "You don't know what I'm thinking," she challenged, practically sneering the words. "And my thoughts are no longer your business."

"Yes, I do. You're spouting a bunch of crap in your head about who you are. Wondering if you should have played the role of helpless female, asking for advice you don't need just so you could stroke my damn ego. But that's not what my leaving was about, and I will not allow you to go there."

Her chest eased from his statement, but she was too worked up to pull back from the edge and find control. Her fingers curled into fists and she pushed at his chest, squirming with pent-up raw emotion. He didn't budge, just moved closer, invading her space and her mind and her body, taking her back to the sizzling connection they always shared, the intensity of their lovemaking an image never far from her mind. "Oh, so you know it all now?" She shot him a furious glare. "You think you have the right to interpret our past the way you see it, and suddenly everything's okay? Well, screw you, Owen. You never gave me a chance! You broke my heart and left me believing I wasn't good enough, so you don't get to tell me anything!"

Pain ravaged his features. His grip softened, his forehead lowered to hers in a humbling embrace that tore her into tiny pieces. A sob broke from her lips. "I'll never forgive myself for hurting you," he whispered. "That's something I'll have to live with."

Her fisted hands opened and slid around his broad shoulders. Her breasts pressed against the hard rock of his chest, causing her nipples to tighten. "I can't do this again. I think I hate you."

She waited for him to retreat, but he pressed a kiss against her temple, ruthlessly gentle while she burned from the inside for more. "I can work with hate. I can dedicate the rest of my life to gaining your forgiveness and trust. I can show you in a thousand different ways how I'll not only treasure you, but push you to be the most magnificent woman you can. Because I'm not afraid of loving you anymore, Chloe."

She gasped, the words tormenting, punishing, and giving her a mad, wild hope he didn't deserve. "Don't you dare."

He cupped her chin, his lips an inch from hers. "I dare. I've dreamed of coming back and doing anything possible to make you love me again. I'm never going anywhere again and I'll prove it. I swear, I'll prove it, babe."

He gave her a few beats to protest.

Chloe got ready to shove him away and run without a glance back.

Instead, she surged forward and pressed her mouth against his.

Shocking heat exploded between them as his lips moved, explored, claimed, with a confidence and power she'd never experienced. This was no shy boy asking permission or the sweet intent of first love morphing into passion. No, this was a determined assault of her senses as his big body pressed against hers, his hands holding her head still while his teeth nipped at her bottom lip with delicious seduction, tempting her to open. She moaned, digging her nails into his shoulders, and his tongue surged forward, possessing her completely.

He kissed with purpose, on the raw edge of control, his tongue tasting, tangling with hers, then plunging deep, not allowing her to hide anymore.

Chloe didn't want to.

She surrendered to the moment and gave in, battling him with her own demands, tilting her hips so his erection notched between her thighs, sliding her fingers up into his hair to tug, pull, and hold him close as he plundered her mouth. The past faded into blurry edges of memory, replaced by a new sexual need screaming for release, and she fell into the kiss with everything she had left, everything she'd always kept only for him.

Slowly, he pulled away, sliding his lips against hers over and over in tiny nips and kisses as if he couldn't stand to leave her. He whispered her name, caressed her hair with slightly trembling fingers, then stared into her eyes.

The truth exploded between them in all its bitter, biting glory.

It was still there.

Worse, it was stronger than before, as if the years between them had allowed the hunger to grow to monstrous proportions. Heart slamming against her ribs, she gazed back at him, too stunned to do anything but utter the first words in her head.

"This is too much."

Heartbreaking tenderness filled his eyes. His thumb traced her slightly swollen lips, still damp from the kiss. "I know."

She blinked and shook her head hard. "It can't work like this. You can't ride in on your white horse, tell me all this stuff, and expect me to drop Drew and just give us another chance. You can't kiss me and believe everything will go back to the way it was. You may have thought of me every night, but I did the opposite. I tried to get you out of my heart and my mind and believed I'd succeeded until you came back. I have a life I built on my own. I'm not about to blow it up because you decided it was a good time for you to return."

He muttered a curse under his breath, but his hands were gentle as they caressed her face. "I needed to tell my truth so you had all the information. So that you realize I'd earmarked my heart for you and never stopped believing we'd get a second chance. How do you feel about Drew?"

She froze. God, she wanted to lie—to hurt like she'd been hurt—but there'd been enough lies between them to last a lifetime. "I don't know. My father adores him."

His laugh held no humor. "Not surprised. Gaining Jonathan's trust back, along with yours, is going to be a challenge." His gaze narrowed with intensity. She fell into the pale, clear blue of his eyes and lost herself there. "But I asked about you. Do you love him?"

"Not yet."

"Good. Then it's not too late." A ghost of a smile fell upon his full lips, hugged by the sexy goatee. She ached to touch his mouth again, trace the line of beard that was both silky and coarse against her skin. "I can try and win you back."

Fear and vulnerability and something else—something true and pure and familiar—rose inside her, twisting in a tangle. "Owen—"

"No, not yet. We talked a lot tonight, and I hit you with too much to process right now. Let me take you home. I'm not going to batter you with my presence or try to push. I'll give you plenty of space and time—I know trust isn't rebuilt with good intentions. It's action. All I ask is you don't force yourself to feel things for Drew because you're afraid of what will happen with us." His mouth firmed into a thin line. "Don't hide from me by running to him, Chloe. Promise me that."

She hesitated, her emotions splintered around her. "I don't think you get to demand anything from me right now."

His laugh surprised her, along with his respectful gaze. "You're right. I can only ask for time. For a chance, on your terms."

She hugged herself, suddenly unsure, and he stepped immediately back. "I'll think about it."

He nodded, taking what he could. "Thank you. Come on, I'll get you home."

They walked back to the table. He paid the bill and drove her back, allowing her the silence in the car to be alone with her thoughts. When he pulled up to her apartment, she waited to see if he'd try to kiss her again or make a passionate plea.

"Good night, Chloe. See you tomorrow."

She raced out of the car and inside her house like demons were chasing her.

And they were.

The ones of the past.

Now she just needed to decide what to do about it.

Chapter Six

The next two weeks passed in a blur of work.

Owen had scored a temporary restraining order to block the Spagarellis from getting any further animals. Most of her days were spent helping him build a solid civil case against the couple by collecting evidence, filing paperwork, and an array of other activities. He kept his word and didn't push, keeping his focus on the job, but slowly, she began to fall again in a whole new way for Owen Salt.

She liked watching him in his element. He dealt with people in a direct, kind manner, able to sift through massive amounts of dialogue or material to find the gold nuggets needed to truly understand. He'd always loved animals, but that had grown into a steady determination to do the best he could for the ones who had no voice. His knowledge of the various rescue shelters showed her he knew his stuff. He hadn't just come from California and figured he'd learn New York culture by immersion.

No, he'd done research. He mentioned the big-time players but also knew the core volunteers and treated them exactly the same. He gained everyone's respect by being the first one in the morning and one of the last to leave at night. This wasn't a drop-in case to him. He cared, and that made all the difference.

But it was him as a man that truly haunted her.

She watched him now, his hand unconsciously funneling through his thick hair, suit slightly rumpled, tie a bit askew. He spoke on the phone, his deep voice vibrating with authority. When he caught her staring, he shot her a lopsided grin, acknowledging her presence in a familiar way that had always charmed her. He'd always managed to make her feel seen, even when he was involved in another task.

Owen treated her like a priority. She'd dated many men who sprinkled attention like gifts, as if she'd been blessed to command their full focus. But Chloe had never been comfortable with playing games like hard-to-get. She craved a deep connection within relationships, and though she was able to excel in the role of happy socialite, flitting from crowd to crowd with ease, there wasn't true fulfillment.

Unfortunately, it was another thing she worried about with Drew.

During their phone conversations, he seemed more focused on shallow subjects rather than her inner passions. Then again, maybe it was too short of a time to judge him. They were still figuring each other out. She planned to attend his financial dinner tomorrow night, so hopefully they'd either grow closer or she'd have to make a hard decision.

Because she couldn't stop thinking about Owen and the kiss.

The office line rang, and she grabbed it, relieved for the distraction. "Advocates for Animals."

"Chloe? It's Viv. I need a favor."

She frowned. "You sound terrible, are you sick?"

A round of coughing echoed over the phone. "Hell, yes. I got the crud so I'm bed bound. Is Owen there?"

"Yeah. Can I come over and help? Bring you soup? Who's helping?"

"No, don't worry, I got my sister being my bitch right now." Chloe heard a faint curse in the background, then a weak laugh. "Let's just say I'm gaining some revenge while she picks up my used tissues. Listen, I need you to take my place at the Sidewalk Angels party tonight. Bring Owen."

She shook her head, thoughts battering together. She'd been looking forward to an evening to catch up on some rest with a pizza delivery box and some serious Netflix bingeing. Now she'd be squeezing into heels, a bra, and dealing with her confusing feelings for her ex. "I can handle it, Viv. Probably no reason to bother Owen—he's only involved with legal, right?"

"That's exactly why I need his presence. Can you put him on speaker?"

Chloe glanced over and found him watching her, head cocked from overhearing his name mentioned. He'd hung up from his phone call. "Need me?"

She swallowed and nodded. "Yeah, Viv needs you to come with me to a function for Sidewalk Angels tonight. Here, she wants to talk to you."

Chloe hit the button.

"Owen! I need you to save my life tonight. I'm stuck in bed, looking like death, and I need you to go with Chloe to this function. I know you're just a loaner from the Animal Defense Fund, but you'd be doing me a favor. I heard there's going to be some big sponsors and donors who want to help us fight more legal cases. Having you by Chloe's side to answer questions, charm them, and show we really care about prosecuting the bastards—not just saving the animals—is important."

"Sure, Vivian, I can attend tonight. Is it formal dress?"

"Cocktail appropriate, so a suit and tie is all you need. Thanks for saving my ass. You, too, Chloe."

"No problem," Chloe said. "Send me the invite with the deets."

"Done. Air hugs—talk later."

Viv hung up.

Chloe swiveled her head around. Owen stared back with a gleam of pleasure in his eyes, even as his lips twitched. "Guess I get another date."

She blew out a breath and tried not to smile back. This upcoming weekend was turning out to be more work than she'd intended—and with two different men. "It's a business function," she corrected. "No kissing."

Oh, God. She shouldn't have said it. Her skin turned warm, and she watched his gaze narrow with interest, satisfaction carving out the lines of his face. "Glad to know you can't get it out of your mind, either," he murmured.

"I can't! I mean, I can. Stop trying to distract me. We have a ton to do before we have to leave."

"You mentioned the kissing. Who's distracting who?"

She shot him a glare. "Forget it."

"I can't. That's my problem also. Wait till I raise the stakes to other things besides kissing. We're doomed."

Frustration mingled with laughter at his mischievous wink, but he strolled away before she could say anything. He'd always loved teasing her and knew exactly how to reduce the tension when a moment got too dark or negative. There was an inner light inside him she'd always been aware of.

She just hadn't known how much she'd missed it until now.

The day flew by, and soon she was transforming herself for the evening. She decided on a classic black dress that hugged her body and had criss-cross halter straps over the shoulders. Shooting a longing glance at her fluffy slippers, she surrendered and chose her treasured and only pair of sparkly Louboutins. If she was going to suffer, it might as well be worth it.

She was on time when Owen buzzed in, despising any sort of lateness—another gift from her father. Grabbing a light wrap, she made her way downstairs to the lobby.

Owen was chatting with the doorman. Her gaze quickly roved over his sleek black suit, admiring the way the fabric emphasized the broadness of his shoulders, but when he turned, all she could do was stop and stare.

Those pale blue eyes filled with a fierce hunger and male appreciation that made shivers explode all over her body. Taking in every detail of her outfit, he straightened and prowled over, closing the distance, then leaned in to whisper in her ear.

"You stun me."

The words hit her full force. She'd received endless compliments from male admirers. Dates. The press. Her friends. Chloe had grown into her confidence, and knew her looks were striking with her dark hair and blue eyes. Being in the public eye made her work a bit harder to always seem flawless, though it was a complete façade. But the way Owen spoke was different. It was as if he not only acknowledged the physical, but also the core of who she was. She fought to reach out and touch him, slide her fingers into his and surrender. Instead, she blinked back the ridiculous sting of tears from his compliment and smiled.

"Thank you. You're looking quite dapper yourself."

He laughed. "For now. By mid-evening, I'll probably have spilled something on myself."

She laughed with him. He'd always been a bit clumsy, but to her, it was part of his charm. Secretly, she was glad he hadn't outgrown it and turned into a polished, perfect suit like so many liked to portray. She preferred flaws in all their glory.

So far, she hadn't discovered any of Drew's. But maybe it was too early.

Chloe pushed the thought out of her mind and followed Owen to the car.

"Want to give me a rundown on anyone I need to dazzle?" he asked, easing into the crowded city streets.

"Marisol and Rob Thomas will be there, of course. They own Sidewalk Angels and donate to a variety of shelters—we received a hefty contribution last year, but hoping there will be a few investors who don't know how we work. We need to grab their ear."

"Got it. His music rocks. Any politicians?"

She rolled her eyes. "No, thank goodness."

He laughed. "Come on, your dad is one of the good guys."

"Yes, but many of them aren't. I never realized how power is more attractive than money to some people. The more they get, the more they crave, and suddenly it's all about what they can get out of an exchange. I give my dad credit that he fights for what he believes in, but I wouldn't want to be part of that world. Alyssa is perfect for him."

"Yes, I was happy to hear he got married again. Even happier when I knew you loved her as part of your family."

She arched a brow. "How did you know that?"

He shrugged. "Harper told me. Sent me pics of the wedding. It was obvious from your smile."

Chloe shifted in her seat. "I don't know if I like the idea you've been keeping tabs on me from across the country. It's weird."

"Sorry, I didn't want to be a stalker. I just wanted to share a piece of your life and know you were okay."

She was silent for a while, mulling over his words. "I can't shift so quickly into believing you cared about me. I've spent too long convincing myself you were a cheating, lying asshole."

A laugh boomed out and she relaxed back in the seat. "Fair enough. Right now, I'm grateful I get to spend another evening in your company. Even better, I get to watch you in action."

They drove into Tribeca, pulled up to the valet, and she exited the car to a sea of flashbulbs. Damn, she'd hoped this was small enough not to warrant press, but it seemed they knew she'd attend. The pack descended, throwing questions out as she tried to move slowly, keeping her smile bright and not looking forced.

"Chloe—what's your take on the governor's decision to cut the budget for educational expenditures?"

"Chloe—why weren't you involved in the protests for Green Farms? Several people were arrested—did you disagree with their stance on humane treatment for farm animals?"

"Chloe—what designer are you wearing tonight?"

"Chloe—are you still seeing Drew Dinkle? Is this your new date?"

The questions peppered like bullets, but she paused briefly, looking into the cameras with practiced poise. "I think you'd find the governor's position on education has always been supportive. He's not cutting the budget, he's moving more to online resources to be able to serve the schools in a changing environment. Advocates for Animals has a long-standing commitment to the ethical treatment of farm animals and has already filed suit against Green Farms." She smiled, tilting her head slightly toward the camera. "And I'm wearing one of my favorite designers, à la Marshalls, off the rack. Now if you'll excuse me."

She pivoted on her red heel and entered the doors, while the reporters kept calling out questions.

"Is it always like that?" he asked, his hand cupping her elbow as they climbed the carpeted staircase to the main dining room.

"Usually. It got worse after that awful magazine came out, naming me the Bachelorette of NYC. Ugh, who would've thought so many people read that trash?"

He cut her an admiring glance. "No man needs to read an article to know you're the catch of the century, babe. I think it's more than a miracle you're still single."

"What could be bigger than a miracle?" she quipped, moving toward the Tribeca Rooftop, where the gala was held.

They stepped out of the elevator and toward the table registering guests and checking invites. He stood close, and his fingers brushed hers, eliciting a tingle that shot through her whole body. "Fate. You were fated for me."

She didn't have time to respond. Chloe recited their names, and they were greeted with genuine warmth and led out to the magnificent terrace. Low, comfortable couches filled the space, along with a full bar and tables displaying arrays of cocktail foods. The beautifully dressed crowd mingled in various groups, and a large screen flashed pictures of the animals Sidewalk Foundation had helped, with dozens of local rescues covering upstate and the city of New York. It was a perfect evening for an outdoor party—the air warm but not too muggy, the sky a velvet ribbon dotted with star studs, and the brilliant city skyline sprawled before them in all its glory.

Owen caught his breath, his gaze sweeping over the city. Pride etched his face, as if he relished the feeling of being a native New Yorker and bearing witness to the grit, grime, and beauty of one of the most powerful cities in the world. It was an emotion Chloe recognized well. It was the reason her father pursued politics with a natural zeal; the purpose of why she wanted to make it a better a place for the animals who lived here. Realizing Owen held the same type of passion for the state he'd grown up in touched her. He belonged to this world, too.

And for Chloe, it was an important element she'd always wanted in a partner.

"I've missed this," Owen murmured, a smile curving his lips. "I knew early on I'd never be a surfer or a true Californian. I enjoyed my time for what it was, but this is where I need to be."

"Me, too. I'd planned to settle closer to the Bishop farm in the Hudson Valley, but I kept being pulled to work in the city. It seemed to call to me—there just aren't enough shelters with the amount of abuse and neglect cases increasing. Plus, we initiated a new program to increase fosters."

"I agree. It was another reason the Animal Defense Fund agreed to my transfer. They're hoping to get some new laws in effect to strengthen penalties—especially pit bull and cock fighting rings."

Her eyes widened. "That's wonderful news. We could use all the legal help we can get. Vivian is always understaffed."

"Another good reason to mingle and share our cause. Shall we?"

He held out an arm.

She took it without hesitation, reminding herself it was good for business.

Chloe ignored her softly sighing heart as he led her into the crowd.

Chapter Seven

Tonight seemed different.

Owen watched her shine, her tangible, positive energy flowing from her aura, urging everyone in her circle to get closer. He didn't blame them. He'd been like a moth attracted to her light since the moment he'd met her, but now he enjoyed watching her thrive in the element she was meant for.

They made a great team. Between his legal knowledge and practical skill, combined with her ability to sell the Advocates for Animals group to people who didn't know about their cause, toward the end of the evening they'd collected a few powerful contacts. The Spagarelli case was big, and many groups were grateful the organization was going hard for the civil suit—too many were easily dropped because of the overwhelming amount of cases.

He sipped champagne, nibbled on appetizers, and enjoyed Chloe's company. After the presentation, and a few live songs from Rob Thomas, music was piped in for some dancing. They'd chosen timeless oldies better suited to the older generation. Not his usual alternative style, but he always appreciated the classics loved by his grandfather. *Sinatra. Bennett. Ray Charles. Elvis.*

The memory of Judge Archie Bennett was a twist of love and regret. He wished he'd gotten his act together sooner, but in his mind, his grandfather had been immortal. Owen hoped he was looking down at him with pride, finally witnessing him living a life of both purpose and good-doing. Just like the judge had always dreamed.

A touch on his arm drew him back. "You're thinking of your

grandfather?" she asked softly, eyes gentle.

"How did you know?"

Her head jerked slightly. "Didn't he love *Can't Help Falling in Love with You?*"

"Yes. I can't believe you remembered that."

She smiled. "You used to tell me how he'd blast his music on the record player until you wanted to cry. That he refused to wear hearing aids so he'd turn it up."

Owen laughed. "I was the only teenager to know every lyric of *Georgia* by Ray Charles. I asked for noise cancelling headphones for Christmas because I couldn't take it anymore."

"It must've been nice, though. Living with your grandpa."

He nodded. "It was. I know I complained a lot, but looking back, I learned so much from him. He was tough but fair and never treated me like my opinions were meaningless. He always listened."

"I love that your mom invited him to stay with you both. It must have helped him to be around family."

"Actually, my mom needed him. There was no way we could keep the house with her salary. Grandpa pretty much payed the rent."

"I think it was a mutually beneficial experience," she said. "He'd be lonely without you both, and you cared for him in his old age. I'd say you both won."

He touched her cheek, grateful for the way she allowed him to see things, then dropped his hand like he'd been burned. Owen didn't want anyone to start any gossip she didn't need, and being together at this function could have stirred up some chatter. He might not want her to date Drew, but he also didn't want to add to her stress. His voice came out ragged. "Sorry. Old habits to break. I know I lost the right to touch you."

A strange expression flickered over her face. He held his breath at the glimpse of longing in her vivid blue eyes, but it was gone so quickly he wondered if he'd imagined it. "It's okay. Let me introduce you to Regina at Rescue Dogs Furever."

Regina was a birdlike woman with a long face and curly black hair that exploded around her head. Dark eyes regarded him with a cynical suspicion, as if she already suspected he'd disappoint her. He pegged her for early sixties. She wore a T-shirt type dress with dogs stamped over it, high strappy black heels, and carried a beaded black bag. Chloe made the introductions, and Regina turned toward him. Her voice held a biting sharpness. "Do you believe you can make the civil suit stick? Or is another abuser going to walk, go to the nearest pet store, and buy more animals to fill up her house again?"

"I'm here to make sure we get our day in court," he said mildly, understanding her frustration. Animal law caused too many people to lose faith, in both the system and humanity. "We have a strong case, and if we can't get her in jail, we'll try to break her financially. Or at least make sure she can't hoard more victims. I was able to get the temporary restraining order, so that was a turning point."

She shook her head, and silver sequined earrings in the shape of tassels swung back and forth. "I just wish the courts would take these issues more seriously. They need bigger penalties. They need some damn judges who don't throw the cases out! Or lawyers who don't give up so easily."

"Agreed," he said. "Animal welfare isn't the most popular segment of law. It doesn't pay as well, and it's definitely not glamorous, but the people who are involved give it their all. I'm actually working with the Animal Defense Fund to provide more education at the colleges and local level. Kids don't know about the job opportunities for rescue, including law. I've signed on to speak in the fall to a bunch of schools to get them useful information on career fields."

Regina stared at him for a while. Her face seemed to yield to a bit of softness. "A good idea," she finally said. "We need better recruiting. And some damn legal support from lawyers who don't look at our organization as some goodwill not-for-profit. We're doing serious work. Hell, I just inherited a bunch of dogs from a puppy mill. Poor mamas never even saw grass—they were trapped in a cage being consistently bred. We'd love to shut that mill down permanently."

Chloe jumped in. "I have some spots I can help fill with some of my fosters. Will that help?"

Regina nodded. "More than you know."

"I may also be able to help," Owen said. "I can reach out to my organization and see if we can assist with the case. We've been trying to exploit more mills—did the press get a hold of the story yet?"

"No, this was kept quiet," Regina said.

"Blow it up." Chloe and Regina regarded him with surprise. "Press is known to get us more supporters—the more noise the better with these cases. Do you know any reporters who'd jump on this type of story?"

"I've got a reporter at Huffpost who covers these cases—I'll contact her," Chloe said quickly.

"Good. And encourage pictures. It feels like exploitation, but this is the good kind—the more people see, the better they react, and that sometimes causes a cry for change," Owen said.

Regina nodded, regarding him with a gleam of respect. Owen felt like he'd climbed a mountain. Something told him this woman didn't like too many people—another human loss from volunteers who'd seen too much evil from the human race. "Thanks. I'll contact you both tomorrow." She glanced at both of them. "You two are a power couple. The kind we need more of." They chatted for a while longer before Regina got called away. When he faced Chloe, she was smiling.

"You charmed her. Very few do."

He cocked his head. "Why? She runs a thriving shelter and wears dog clothes. That's my kind of woman."

He relished her laughter, the sound like tinkling bells in his ears. "She's had some run-ins with men who don't take her seriously. Let's just say lawyers are not her favorite."

"Then I'm glad I get the opportunity to change her mind."

She was looking at him like she used to. His heart hammered hard in his chest, and it took all his willpower not to move closer, cup her chin, press his lips to hers, and ease into the kiss they were both craving. He stood his ground, fighting impulse, and then Fate took a hand and changed everything.

The strains of the smoky, rich melody poured over the speakers. They both froze, the song as familiar as breath, haunting as a misty dream that made him ache all over. Couples moved to dance under the star-streaked night sky, and he stared at her, caught between the memories of the past and his fantasies for the future.

His gaze drilled into hers. "Dance with me."

Her lips parted. "I don't think we should."

Owen moved on pure impulse, driven to hold her once again, while Etta James crooned *At Last* and spun them into a magical web. He reached out his hand to her. "Dance with me, Chloe," he repeated.

He waited, half expecting her to walk away, leaving him alone, his hand reaching out to only empty space and a past he couldn't overcome.

Her body shuddered as she dragged in a breath.

She placed her hand in his. He led her a few steps to the open space and gently took her into his arms.

The scent of wildflowers and sunshine filled his nostrils, and within moments, she'd settled against him with a naturalness confirming she'd always belonged to him. He lowered his head to her ear, his arms wrapped around her lithe body like a lover rather than co-worker or friend. The world fell away, and he was once again at the wedding. They'd been dancing and laughing to Prince, having fun on the floor, until Etta James suddenly belted out her rich, sexy voice, singing about a forever love under a night sky. Awkward, shaky with the need of a teen desperately crushing on a girl of his dreams, he'd reached out his hands in invitation, and she'd stepped into his arms.

"I always wondered why you said yes to that dance," he murmured, pressing his palm to the small of her back. "You never seemed interested before. Treated me like a younger brother. Yet, suddenly I got to hold you, and I was never the same again."

A tiny gasp escaped her lips. She tilted her head up and their cheeks brushed. Her grip tightened on his shoulders and he tamped down a groan as the fire hit his body and exploded in tiny licks of flame. "I don't know. I always liked you, but it was never romantically until that dance. The way you looked at me with your heart in your eyes. The gentleness in how you touched me. And then you said—"

"Thank you for this past summer. You changed me, and any guy who doesn't treat you like the best thing he has doesn't deserve you."

She stumbled. He eased her closer. "Yes."

"I was so clumsy with words. I finally managed to ask you out by the end of the song. I can't believe you agreed to go on a date," he said.

"It wasn't what you said, Owen. It was the way you said it. Like you really meant it. Like I was special."

He pressed his lips against her temple. "Because you were. You are. Knowing I made you question that by leaving will haunt me forever."

The last of her resistance faded and she melted against him. His thighs brushed hers. Her breasts pushed against the wall of his chest. His lips coasted over her face in light brushes as they fell into the song, into the night, into each other. Time slowed, stilled, stopped. Light streaked the sky, Etta James crooned about finding the one, and Owen tumbled all over again, on this night, in this moment, holding the woman he'd always loved and always would.

When the song ended, he stepped back, still holding her hand. Her blue eyes were wide, a bit stunned, as if she'd experienced the same emotions. Wild hope surged and shook through him. God, he wanted her. Needed her. He whispered her name, sensing she was on the verge of giving him back a part of herself, of giving him a second chance to protect her heart.

Instead, she slowly retreated, her hand slipping from his grasp. The wall slammed down between them, and Chloe turned away, shoulders squared as if leaving a battle she'd just barely won. "It's late. I think we better go. I need to hit the rest room, I'll meet you downstairs."

"Chloe—"

Her name hung on the breeze as she walked away from him.

Chapter Eight

The flowers came the next day. This time, the blooms were a rich, creamy white, looking almost like an Instagram photo, the open petals tinged with a touch of dusty pink. The vase was square and crystal cut. The card read, *Can't wait for tonight.*

This time, Owen didn't mention the delivery. He kept his distance, immediately launching into work mode and trying to catch up on the leads they'd been given from last night's fundraiser. He'd already contacted the Animal Defense Fund and agreed to get help for Regina and the puppy mill case.

Chloe went through the motions and tried to convince herself it was for the best. Last night had been too intense. Dancing with him to their song created a storm of emotion inside. Her mind blurred and her body came alive, practically zinging under every stroke of his hands, glide of his hips, and burning stare that reminded her of how good it had been between them.

Until it had gone bad.

Her instincts screamed for her to run when the song ended before he could utter words she wasn't ready to hear. Owen had followed her lead and drove her home in relative silence. But his gaze haunted her in her dreams, along with the kiss she still couldn't forget.

Tonight, she had her big date with Drew. Chloe wanted to give him the chance he deserved. It wasn't fair for her not to explore their relationship, especially since she'd worked so hard to put Owen in the past. But a part of her also recognized tonight was a test. She wasn't a game player. If she wasn't experiencing the seeds for growth in their relationship, Chloe would end it. It wasn't fair to lead either Drew or Owen to play them off one another.

She sensed Owen knew she'd be seeing Drew tonight and decided to back off. God knows, she appreciated the space. Lately, her emotions spun so hard, she only wanted clarity.

Chloe spent the late afternoon at site visits, her favorite part of the job. She checked on her fosters and abused animals settled into local shelters. By the time she'd finished up, she was running late, so she quickly showered and changed, deciding to dress a bit more sophisticated tonight for the Wall Street crowd. Her dress was a silky navy blue that spilled to the floor and left her back bare. She paired it with the sapphire necklace and drop earrings her father had given her last Christmas, slid her feet into platform silver heels, and was thankfully ready when Drew buzzed in.

Casting one last longing look at her slippers and TV, she got ready to dazzle for the evening. He waited outside with his driver, and his gaze lit with appreciation as she walked toward him. "You look beautiful," he said with a smile, flashing a devastating set of dimples. "I'm going to be the luckiest guy in the room."

Chloe smiled back. "Thank you. And I'd say...ditto." He cut a handsome figure in his custom suit, the material emphasizing his trim build and muscles. The expensive Italian shoes were leather. She wondered if they were vegan, then pushed the thought from her mind. Sometimes it was better not to know. Drew liked the finer things in life, which sometimes meant products she refused to purchase in protection of the animals. But now wasn't the time for such a serious dialogue.

He laughed and guided her into the car, where champagne was already chilling. "A pre-cocktail to celebrate."

"Did you close a new deal?"

He poured and handed her a delicate crystal flute. "No, but I get to spend the evening with you so that's a good reason. Did you like the flowers?"

She shifted in her seat. "Yes, I texted you. They're stunning."

"Roses remind me of you. There's a classic mystery to them I always enjoyed, and of course, timeless elegance."

She gave him points for the description, even if he'd never thought to just ask what flowers she enjoyed. She was used to dealing with alpha men, though, especially in the world her father walked in, so Chloe had no problem holding her own. "How was your week?"

He filled her in on some complex deals she found interesting, and they talked about the economy and predictions with ease. Then Drew paused, resting a palm on her knee, squeezing gently. "I haven't dated many women who were able to discuss finance in depth. It's refreshing."

"I took a lot of economics courses. My father always said history and the economy is something we need to learn from due to concrete patterns that play out."

"Brains and beauty. I'm going to have to step up my game so I don't lose you."

She frowned at the odd statement. "What do you mean?"

Drew hesitated. "I saw a photo from last night's event. Is he someone I need to worry about?"

She jerked slightly. Dammit, of course it was in the press. They usually ignored her responses to hard questions, and focused on their speculation of whether her escorts were professional or personal. Drew had been mentioned a lot these past weeks as her current love interest. "Owen's working with me on the Spagarelli case," she said, wondering how much truth to give him. "Vivian got sick and asked him to accompany me."

He let out a breath, his face relaxed. "Got it. I didn't mean to push; I know we never spoke of dating exclusively. I just wanted to know if I had competition."

She opened her mouth to explain a bit more about their shared past, but they'd suddenly arrived. Drew spoke to the driver, and she was whisked inside to a private room.

The elegant French restaurant was known for its cutting-edge menu, elegant décor, and exorbitant prices. Personally, she preferred her food presented in larger portions, but she was already impressed with the long banquet table decorated with snowy white china, sparkling crystal, and low bowls of cream-colored flowers floating in water. The floor to ceiling windows overlooked the gardens, where couples were already mingling, strolling with drinks in hand.

Drew took her hand. His grip was warm and firm. "I can't wait to show you off," he said with a sexy wink, leading her to the terrace.

Once again, she wondered why it seemed she was always referenced as an object to brag about. Of course, he probably meant it as a compliment, but her looks were the thing she cared the least about, even as someone in the public eye. Her most cherished moments were spent in jeans and T-shirt with dirty sneakers, covered in dog hair. Drew definitely preferred the spotlight of well-attended functions and loved to share stories of who he met when he was out, along with the most popular new venues in the city.

Not that there was anything wrong with being social. It was a good thing.

She put her smile to full-power and spent the next hour sipping wine and getting to know the roughly dozen of his staff. They were all men, which surprised her. Drew seemed to respect women, and she'd expected more females in high-powered positions. The more time she spent chatting, the more she realized how different the men's companions were.

Chloe was used to cliques in high society, so when she'd found her tribe with animal rescue, it was as if she could finally relax into being herself. But the women's judging gazes on her dress, her shoes, her bag, and the pointless questions about where she lived and what it was like to be the governor's daughter left her cold. No one held a job, and they seemed to be most concerned with how they looked to one another, and especially to their husbands or lovers. They spoke of tennis and golf, places to lunch, names of popular stylists and home designers, and skimmed the surface of any true conversation.

By the time they sat down to dinner, Drew seemed to be holding court. They laughed at his jokes, complimented him on the last deal he'd closed, and basically kissed his ass. Chloe felt as if she was stuck at a political dinner except occasionally her father would shoot her a suffering, sorry look and make her laugh. They'd agreed there had always been too many large egos in politics. Her dad taught her real power was not in leading but by serving because that was where the real work was done. It was obvious at this table Drew was king and enjoyed ruling his team.

"Chloe, I find it amazing you're such a crusader. It's so refreshing," Emma gushed to her right, platinum blonde hair pulled high on top of her head in a model-like pony. The style emphasized the smooth skin, wrinkle-free, pulled tight over her face. "I had to quit so many of my charities once Brett got promoted. There was so much to do all the time, and of course, now we're trying to get pregnant so I'll be super busy."

Chloe tilted her head. "Well, it's my actual job I get paid for," she said, trying not to roll her eyes. "I'm not volunteering at a charity, but thank God for all our volunteers or we'd never be able to do the work needed."

Drew grinned from the head of the table, shooting Chloe a look of adoration. "My girlfriend wants to save the world, one animal at a time.

She's going to do big things for the Foundation one day."

Chloe tried not to wince at the term. They'd never discussed dating exclusively and she didn't feel comfortable with being called his girlfriend. But she couldn't call him out here. "That's right, you give a lot to those rescue places, don't you?" Brett asked. "I had a dog when I was growing up. German shepherd. One of the smartest breeds—she was my best friend."

The crowd sighed and made little sounds of approval. "Advocates for Animals does much more than rescue. We're currently in a civil action suit trying to shut down a hoarding situation. We get involved in closing down puppy mills, pit bull fighting rings, and dozens of other causes that need attention."

Drew nodded. "Chloe takes her work seriously. Can you imagine what type of mother she'll make?"

"Drew, I've never seen you like this. You're positively adorable," Sarah drawled from across the table. Her husband, Adam, was Drew's right hand, and they were obviously a power couple. The whole time Chloe was speaking with them, she was regaled with tales of expensive vacations that took place on safari expeditions and sleek yachts.

Adam laughed. "You got it bad, buddy. Nice to see a woman who may finally tame you. It's time for you to join our club—we've been needing new members."

Horror slowly trickled over her as Chloe witnessed herself being talked about like she wasn't here. Had Adam literally hinted at marriage? And had Drew actually mentioned she'd be a good mother, like he was parading her out for opinions? She waited for Drew's answer, hoping he'd save the situation, but instead, he shot her a wink. "I've gotten to this point by going after what I want without fear. Love should be looked at the same, don't you think?"

The group enthusiastically agreed, citing Drew's bravery for putting himself out there, and that Chloe was a lucky woman. No one bothered to ask her about their relationship. Hell, it seemed she was just supposed to shut her mouth, look pretty, and agree.

Chloe glanced at her watch, wondering when she could go home.

Coffee and dessert followed, but she noticed it was a light sorbet with no calories, and most of the women groaned and mentioned their designer dresses or not-yet-pregnant bellies for the reason most were left behind.

She ate and relished every last bite.

Finally, they finished up and walked out. Drew held her hand and she let him. Chloe air kissed all six of the women who promised to ping her online about getting together, and she never broke her stride or her smile. They'd just reached the sidewalk where Drew's car waited when the lightbulbs flashed in her face.

"Chloe—are you dating two different men?"

"Chloe—was this evening for another fundraiser or personal?"

"Drew—what's it like dating the most famous bachelorette in the city?"

She grit her teeth and suffocated the scream that wanted to rip from her mouth. How had they known she was here? This was not a good time to be bombarded, especially when Drew held her hand, even when she tried to gently tug away from his grip. Before she could say a word, Drew turned toward the group of paparazzi and gave a charming grin.

"This was a private dinner I hosted for my team at D&D Finance Investments. Chloe was kind enough to accompany me. As for how it feels to date one of the most beautiful, accomplished women in New York?" He beamed down at her. "It's pretty damn awesome."

Laughter rose up. More questions attacked her from all ends, along with the cameras. She tried to ease toward the open door of the car, pulling him with her, and the rest seemed to happen in slow motion.

Drew stepped in, bent over, and kissed her.

Bulbs exploded.

The kiss was short, leaving her staring at him in shock. He turned and gave his sexy wink to the reporters. "If you'll excuse us, it's time for us to have some needed privacy," Drew announced. "Come on, sweetheart."

She slid into her seat and the door closed. He must've said something else, because there was a few more flashes, then Drew climbed into the other side, motioning for his driver to go.

He shot her a warm glance, obviously not understanding the reason for her icy silence. "Well, that was fun. Everyone adored you, just like I knew they would. Did you have a good time?"

Endless responses swirled in her brain, but she wondered if they'd been on different pages this whole time. Drew wasn't what she'd thought. He wasn't a bad man, and she bet many women would love to be pampered and adored by him.

He just wasn't the man for her.

"Drew, why did you kiss me in front of those reporters?" she asked.

His brow marred in obvious confusion. "I wanted to show them I was serious about you. That we're a couple."

Her temples suddenly throbbed and a bone weariness overcame her. "I'm sorry, I think we may have misunderstood each other. I've had a wonderful time with you, but I don't feel like we're right for each other."

He blinked. "You can't be serious, Chloe. Each of our dates have gotten better. We make an incredible team—we have the same interests, and I'm crazy about you. We have chemistry, and you've seemed happy with me this past month. Did something happen?"

"No." She sighed. Yes, Owen had forced her to question her feelings for Drew, but she knew in her gut she would have figured that out on her own. Owen coming back had only expedited the process. "I don't love you."

"Not yet, but we were getting there. Why would you want to run away before giving us a chance?"

She gazed at him with sadness. God, had he really fallen for her? Or was he more disappointed in a missed opportunity to find a woman who fit his ideals? She hated the idea of hurting him, but it couldn't go on anymore. Not when she knew the result. "I did give it a chance," she said quietly. "My heart just isn't for you. I think it's best to stop seeing each other. I really hope you can understand and respect my decision. I never wanted to hurt you, Drew."

His gaze narrowed slightly. "Is it that guy you were with last night? The one you said was only business?"

"Owen and I used to date years back, but it's not the reason I'm breaking this off with you."

He seemed to process her words like an analytical spreadsheet. "I see. Did Owen say he wants you back?"

Shit.

Chloe owed him the truth, even though it was uncomfortable. "Yes. But I don't know what will happen with us. There's a lot of history I'm not sure I can get past. I'm being honest, Owen has nothing to do with my decision. But I do know it's best we end it here. I hope we can be friends."

She held her breath and hoped he didn't push.

Drew shook his head and gave a halfhearted laugh. "Friends, huh? The biggest rejection of all, other than 'it's me, not you.'"

She winced. "I didn't want to hurt you."

The car pulled up to her apartment building. He let out a breath, then nodded. "I know. But listen, I think you're confused right now with this guy coming back. He's an asshole, Chloe. I would've never left or hurt you if you were mine."

Her heart ached. Drew was right, but she knew after speaking with Owen it was more complicated than black and white. She'd always believed it would be easy to walk away if she saw Owen again, but only after two short weeks, real feelings were involved. She needed more time to make a decision if Owen and she still had a future, but either way, she knew Drew was not meant for her.

Drew touched her arm. "Take some time and space. I'll be here if you change your mind."

Chloe climbed out of the car. With every step farther, she confirmed she'd made the right decision. No matter how hard her head wanted it to work out with Drew, her soul sensed they weren't meant to be. She was okay with that.

Her father?

Maybe not so much. Especially after he learned she might need to explore a second chance with Owen. But Alyssa would help soothe his protective instincts, and Chloe knew how to take care of herself.

She got to her place, changed into her pj's, and finally had a dreamless, sleep-filled night.

Chapter Nine

The moment Owen saw the roses, he knew it was going to be a bad day.

He'd been hopeful to hear from Chloe over the weekend, but she'd remained silent. After their evening together, he felt they'd made progress. When he looked into her eyes, he knew in his gut she still had strong feelings. The connection between them hadn't been severed—only bent. He'd spent the weekend tying up loose ends on the case and reaching out to some old friends to grab a beer and catch up. The rest of the time he thought about Chloe and his next move.

Until he arrived Monday morning to the flowers. And the card.

This time, there was no envelope. Just a fancy notecard with one line written in elegant scrawl.

Can't Stop Thinking About Our Night Together.

The punch in his gut was brutal. She'd seen *him* this weekend. Even worse, they could have spent the night together. The idea of the woman he loved being in another man's arms made him nauseous. Frustration warred with a deep-set panic at the idea of losing her all over again. He'd googled everything about Drew Dinkle. He looked like fucking Captain America, which sucked, but even worse? He was rich, self-made, and owned a foundation that helped the animals. He was everything Chloe was meant for—all the things Owen had wanted to become when he was a nineteen-year-old kid, dreaming of spending his life with his first love.

And he wondered again, was he enough?

Vivian came into the office, interrupting his thoughts. "Morning, Owen. What's the update on our case?"

He forced a smile and re-focused. "We were assigned our court date six weeks from now. We'll be ready. I have to head to the courthouse today. How do you feel?"

"Much better, thanks. I received a few phone calls from the Sidewalk Angels event. You did a great job. Regina was really appreciative of your help."

"I'm glad. I'm reaching out to a few of my contacts who are versed on puppy mills. I told Regina to blow it up in the press."

Vivian gave a shark-like smile. "Excellent advice. You're doing great—I wish I could steal you for Advocates for Animals full-time. You and Chloe make a deadly team."

He ignored the ache in his chest and nodded. "Is she coming in today?" he asked casually.

"She's at a site visit this morning. Oh, is that the new delivery?" Vivian headed to Chloe's desk and smelled the roses. "Seems like Captain America finally captured her. So damn romantic, but Lord knows that girl deserves her happy ever after. Plus, Drew's working on a large funding for us which we desperately need. Guess it's a win/win."

"They're serious, huh?" he asked.

Vivian laughed. "Hope so. They're perfect for each other. Better get to work, I'll see you later."

She left and he spent the next few hours on some other cases the Animal Defense Fund needed his help on. By the time he reached the courthouse, it was past lunch and he'd managed to numb his emotions. He greeted Mario, a savvy lawyer who worked for one of the larger firms focused on animal rights. The firm was making a name for itself in the community, and Mario was one of the good guys. His tall, dark good looks only added to his lethalness in the courtroom. "Owen, good to see you, man. You're working on Spagarelli, right?"

"Yes, we're on the docket for next month. Been wanting to reach out to set up a lunch date."

"Funny you should mention that. Your name's been floating around my office lately as a potential recruit."

Owen looked at him with surprise. "Didn't think you were expanding."

"Only for the right people. You've done great things with the Animal Defense Fund. We need another decent lawyer on our team. Interested?"

He hesitated. Working for a not-for-profit didn't pay as well as the private firms, but he was also loyal to the organization that had taken him in and allowed him to learn the law as an intern. "I'm pretty happy where

I'm at."

Mario laughed. "At least hear our pitch. I know the amount of hours you work isn't comparable to the paycheck, and there's little growth. You can be doing some big things with us."

The idea intrigued him. He shifted his briefcase and nodded. "Let's talk."

Mario bumped his shoulder. "Good. We don't even mind the scandal. I see you've been busy since you hit our city. You work fast, man."

He cocked his head, confused. "What are you talking about?"

Mario lifted a dark brow. "Page Six, man. You're splashed all over the paper today. A love triangle with the governor's daughter is pretty juicy. Don't tell me you didn't know."

His blood chilled. A sense of foreboding washed over him, but he pushed himself to ask. "You have a copy?"

"Sure, my girlfriend was gushing about how romantic it all was this morning. Here you go, keep it. I better head in. I'll call you for lunch."

Owen nodded, his hands slightly trembling as he flicked open the page.

GOVERNOR'S DAUGHTER CAUGHT IN LOVE TRIANGLE! WHICH MAN WILL STEAL HER HEART FOREVER?

He stared at the two pictures side by side. The first was a shot of them dancing together on the rooftop. Someone must've taken the photo from their phone—it was a bit grainy but the way he stared down at Chloe, holding her tight, clearly showed he was interested in more than business. The way she clutched him close and pressed her face into his shoulder gave off romantic vibes.

The second picture slammed him like a sucker punch. Drew was kissing Chloe, her face upturned as she leaned against the car door, snug against him. He stared at it for a long time as his insides slowly broke apart and the realization finally trickled through him.

He was too late.

She was falling for her perfect superhero. Owen couldn't compete with the ideal of who he'd always believed she was meant to be with. The familiar demons whispered in his ear, reminding him it was best to bow out and leave her to be happy.

He crumpled the paper in his hand and walked into the courtroom, trying to decide what he was going to do.

＊＊＊＊

Dear God.

She'd made Page Six.

Chloe sat at her desk with the door closed. The roses mocked her with their mysterious message, the cloying scent filling her nostrils. Drew had deliberately left off an envelope. Why was he suddenly playing these games?

The photographs stared up at her in mockery. She was trapped in a nightmare. Sure, she'd made the papers and gossip columns before, but none had been so evidently gleeful of splashing her personal life for the world to see. Her private struggle was now public. Even worse? Advocates for Animals was dragged into the mess because of Owen.

Owen.

What would he think? He had no idea she'd broken up with Drew Friday night. How many times had she dreamed up a revenge to hurt him back, and now all she wanted to do was run and explain. A wave of dizziness hit and she groaned, trying to decide her next step. Already, her phone was blowing up with texts and emails, as more news outlets ran the story in the hunt for gossipy pieces. She had to get ahead of it somehow, by either making a statement, or going into hiding until things blew over.

On cue, her phone blasted the familiar words from Darth Vader.

This is your father.

She closed her eyes halfway and hit the button. "Hi, Dad."

"Did you see Page Six?"

She sighed. "Yep. Now's not a good time to talk. Can I call you later?"

"No. What's going on? Why are you dancing with Owen Salt? Are you involved in a love triangle?"

"No, Dad! Ugh, I went with Owen to a business thing and we danced. Then I had a date with Drew the next night and the paparazzi caught us leaving dinner."

"Oh, okay. So you're happily with Drew and they're just dredging up dirt to exploit. I got your back, honey. I'll have Alyssa begin putting out fires and drop hints that you and Drew are the real thing. How's he taking it?"

"I broke up with Drew that night. We're not together any longer."

A few beats of silence passed. "Is this because of Owen Salt?"

"No. And stop saying his full name like you're about to call a hit on him. Owen made things more complicated, but Drew wasn't the man for me, Dad. I can't explain it—we're just two different people and I didn't want to lead him on. It's for the best."

Her father spoke carefully, as if picking his way through mine field bombs. "Honey, I know this thing blew up for you, but I really think you're letting the past with Owen affect you. I didn't want to tell you this, but Drew texted me this week. He's a really great guy. Told me he wanted to be respectful and that his feelings for you are strong, and he was thinking of moving toward a committed relationship. He mentioned marriage."

"What!"

"I know it's a short time, but maybe you got spooked? Love is scary, especially the right kind. Drew is a grown-up. Owen always struck me as a kid looking for some fun. He's not the type of man you settle down for."

Temper shot through her. "Dad, I'm done with this conversation. Knowing Drew texted you makes me even happier I broke up with him. I may respect you, but this is my life and my decision. You never wanted to get to really know Owen because you kept reminding me it was a first love. Mom was your first. How would you have felt if your feelings were discounted just because of your age?"

A hard breath exhaled over the phone. "This is different."

"No, it's not. I'll handle it my own way."

"Fine. I'm calling for another reason. We need to go to the farm this weekend. Mia invited us up for Evelyn's first birthday party. We can talk, and have some family time away from the madness. God knows I need it, too."

The idea of quiet solace at her favorite place settled her down. "I forgot her birthday's this weekend! Mia mentioned it a while ago. Of course I'll be there."

"Good. Something tells me you need an intervention."

"Dad!"

"Fine, sorry. Are you okay? Can I do anything?"

Her tone softened. Her father was overbearing at times, but she knew it was because he loved her and felt protective, especially after all the ups and downs they'd gone through in their relationship. "No. I'll see you in a few days."

"Love you."

"Love you, too." She hung up and glanced at Owen's empty desk. Was he coming in today? She wanted a chance to talk to him honestly, but another part of her just wanted to hide. Unfortunately, being the governor's daughter in NYC didn't allow her much privacy. Reporters would be stalking her for comments the next few days. Better for her to stay buried in the office and focus on work.

The door burst open. Vivian walked in and stopped before her desk. Dark eyes wide in her face, she stabbed a finger in the air. "Are you sleeping with Owen Salt?"

Chloe groaned. "What is up with everyone using his first and last name?"

"Answer me, girlfriend. I just saw the papers and Owen said nothing to me this morning. What's going on with you two?"

"I'm in a mess, Viv. I never told you I knew Owen before. We were each other's first love."

Vivian dragged over the other desk chair and plopped herself down. "Start from the beginning. Tell me everything."

She did. Her friend listened without interruption, nodding occasionally until Chloe finished with breaking it off with Drew. Viv jerked her head toward the flowers. "So that move was to piss off Owen, I'm assuming?"

"Probably. Makes it sounds like we spent the night together. Drew said he wanted to give me some time, but I already know how I feel. Do you believe he texted my father?"

Vivian rolled her eyes. "Definitely not a Captain America type of move. I can't believe you kept all this so tight. Hell, I can't believe out of all the lawyers in all the world, we picked Owen. Kind of like—"

"Fate?" she finished.

"Yep. What are you going to do?"

"I need to talk to Owen. Tell him what's going on."

"But what do you want, Chloe? Another chance? Do you want to try again with him?"

She sighed. "I'm drawn to him in a way I've never experienced before. And it's just as powerful as when we were young. But I don't know if it's too late for us to pick up all the pieces and begin again."

Vivian nodded. "I hear you. I guess you have to figure it out. Owen's in court so he won't be back today."

"Maybe it's for the best. He'd probably get stalked by reporters around here. I'm sorry, Viv. I never meant to drag everyone into this mess. I hope it doesn't affect any of our donors or staff."

Vivian rose from the chair and laughed. "Are you kidding? Nothing like a good love triangle to get the animals some positive press. Don't worry, we can all handle it. Let me know if you need anything."

"Thanks."

She watched her friend leave, then began sorting through the mess on her desk and blowing up her phone. She'd hole up in her office and get lunch and dinner delivered.

And eventually, talk to Owen.

Chapter Ten

Owen had just opened up a cold beer and checked his phone again to see if Chloe had reached out yet.

Still nothing.

It had been a day from hell, and all he could think about was how she'd probably made her decision to be with Drew.

The buzzer cut into his thoughts and startled him. Maybe she'd come to see him? He hit the intercom. "Yes?"

"Drew Dinkle to see you, sir," the doorman informed.

He jerked back. What the hell? Why was Drew tracking him down? To rub in his victory? Anger flicked at his nerves. He thought of going downstairs to meet him, but figured it would be best to keep the conversation private. "Send him up."

Drew entered his apartment dressed in a tailored, sleek black suit and pink shirt. He smelled of beachy, expensive cologne. His jaw was freshly shaven and perfectly squared. He gazed back at Owen with a cool, clipped disapproval, taking in his sparsely decorated apartment and his worn-out sweats and T-shirt.

"I wanted to talk to you," he said, posture perfectly straight. "About Chloe."

"I figured that'd be the subject." Owen regarded him with a touch of wariness, though he made sure to keep it off his face. "What's up?"

"A few things. First, I came here to ask you man to man to back off. Chloe and I are falling in love. She doesn't need your little games messing with her head."

He arched a brow. Had something else happened between them?

This didn't sound like a confident man showing off. "I'm not here to play any type of games. I've been honest with Chloe about what I want, and that's between the two of us. There's no ring on her finger," he said mildly.

Drew narrowed his gaze. "There will be soon. Let me be direct. You left her once, and deep down, no matter what you do, she'll never trust you again. Women don't let themselves get invested in true second chances with the assholes who dump them. It's textbook."

The words pushed at his own doubts. Could she ever truly forgive him and risk her heart again? "I didn't realize you were a romance expert."

"I intend to marry her. We also know she's passionate about her work. My foundation was about to give Advocates for Animals a sizable donation. Do you really want to be the reason her organization doesn't receive it?"

Shock barreled through him. Was this guy for real? "Are you telling me you'd pull the funds just to get back at me? You'd want to hurt Chloe for a little revenge?"

"Of course not. I'm trying to protect her, and giving you incentive to leave her alone is the only way to do that."

"And if I told her what you were trying to do?" he challenged, temper curling inside him.

Drew shrugged. "I'd deny it. She wouldn't believe you, anyway. You'll never be enough for her, Salt. Look at you. You're still wet behind the ears and no match for the governor's daughter. Jonathan and I are close and will work well together. You have no money and working at a not-for-profit will never be able to support both of you. Chloe deserves to be pampered in style. What do you have to offer her?"

"How about love?"

Drew smirked. "I can offer her that, along with everything else. She'd live like a queen and have an entire foundation to run and help any rescue she wants. Love alone is for naïve teenagers. The real world rewards couples who want to settle down and have a future. To grow into more together. You already gave her your best, and it will never be enough."

In some respect, Owen knew the man was playing a game of words, trying to intimidate like a ruthless business shark intent on closing a deal. As much as he recognized the tactics, the truth hit him full force, barreling into him like a missile shattering his confident façade. Because inside, he still wondered the same exact thing.

Would he ever be enough for Chloe Lake?

"Just back off and leave Chloe alone. It'll be best for everyone involved. I know a lot of people, Salt. I can make things uncomfortable for you here. Besides, you can never truly satisfy her—in bed, or out."

He turned to leave. Drew's words had been chosen to target his weak points, as if the man knew Owen had spent his life trying to be worthy of being the man Chloe Lake loved.

But no longer.

The ego behind Drew's statement revealed a man who loved himself, not Chloe. He wasn't better than Owen just because he had power and money and Jonathan's ear. Because no other man would ever be able to give Chloe what she truly wanted and needed.

Love. Trust. Companionship. Respect.

All the things she deserved.

All the things Drew Dinkle knew nothing about.

Owen used his voice like a whiplash. "You're wrong, dude. On every level."

Drew glanced over, giving him a scathing glare. "Oh, really?"

"Yeah, really. Because you showed your hand the moment you tried to sacrifice the grant in defense of your so-called love for her. You'd be the one to break Chloe's heart, with your selfishness and ego. I'm not going anywhere. Because she deserves better than you."

The man's lips curled back in a sneer. "Then you'll be very, very sorry."

He shut the door behind him.

Owen cursed under his breath. What an asshole. That dialogue ran deeper than a man trying to protect his relationship. That was almost primitive, as if he was trying to desperately get back something he lost.

Maybe it was time to figure out what was really going on.

He grabbed his keys and headed out the door.

Half an hour later, he gazed up at her building and hesitated. Somehow, he'd known he was headed here the entire time.

Owen typed the text and hit send.

I'm outside. Want to talk?

He didn't have to wait long for the answer. *Yes. Come up.*

She was waiting for him at the door. She wore frayed jean shorts and a purple T-shirt that proclaimed, *I Just Want to Rescue Dogs and Drink Wine*. Hair up in a messy bun, feet bare, her face free of makeup, she was simply the most beautiful woman he'd ever seen. Owen stepped inside, glancing around the warm, cozy space that smelled of all the good things he loved.

Freshly cut grass baked in sunshine with a burst of citrus—clean and joyful and pure.

His gaze swept over the room. It was small, as most New York City apartments were, but completely functional. The yellow floral chair and loveseat created a square corner by the TV and bookcase, making it an intimate reading corner. The walls were a pale lemon yellow, and fluffy white rugs were scattered over the wooden floors. She'd always been casually messy, preferring a more relaxed environment, with blankets, knick-knacks, folders, and endless candles set out. The kitchen was a small galley with two pine chairs and table. A bunch of colorful blooms popped out from a yellow mug with a happy face.

Wildflowers.

She hadn't brought the roses home.

Chloe stood in front of him, arms tucked into her elbows, rocking back on her bare heels. He ached to take her into his arms and just hold her. An anxious frown marred her brow. "Did you see any paparazzi out front?"

He shook his head. "I looked before I approached your place." He paused. "Drew came to see me tonight."

Her eyes widened in shock. "What? Oh, my, God, what was he doing there?"

Owen shifted his weight and glanced toward the kitchen. "Long story. Got any beer?"

"Sure." He waited while she retrieved a beer, cracked it open, and handed it over. Their fingers brushed and brought a current of heat around the chilled bottle. She yanked her hand back, then shook her head. "I'm assuming you saw Page Six."

He moved deeper into the room and eased closer to her. "I did."

"I'm sorry you got dragged into this," she finally said. "I'm sure the last thing you need are cameras following you around because of me."

"I'm not sorry. It's part of your life in the spotlight. And that dance was special. Reminded me of all the good things between us."

"Oh." She seemed caught off guard, her fists clenching and unclenching in her normal nervous tell. "What did Drew say?"

He kept his gaze steady and glued to hers. "Let's just say he was clear in his intentions for me to stay away from you."

"I don't like being fought over like a bone," she said with a touch of bitterness.

He arched a brow and took a huge gamble. "It wasn't like that. I think he genuinely believes he's better for you. That he can give you the things I can't. He's got money, a powerful foundation that can do a lot of good for animal rescue, and your father's approval. He's self-made, so he obviously has ambition. And he recognized you for your worth."

Her anger was a beautiful thing to watch, like a frothy cocktail ready to splash over the edges of a glass. She practically growled her words, eyes snapping blue fire. "Wonderful, then it's settled. I guess Drew wins. He checks all the boxes, and you'll surrender me to him gracefully. You always were a gentleman, Owen."

His lips quirked. The fact she was pissed gave him hope. She wasn't in love with Drew. If so, she'd be defending him and pushing Owen away. As bad as she might want to have Drew be the one, it wasn't working. Thank God, because the man was an asshole. "You don't understand, Chloe. I concur his points are reasonable and may be true, but it means nothing to me. I'm not stepping politely away because I think he's better than me. That's my point—it's the exact reason I needed to leave four years ago. The Drews in the world would have beaten me every time. I didn't believe in myself back then. But now?" He leaned in, catching her scent, the air practically crackling around them. "Let's just say I'll go to the mattresses for you, babe. I'm the man for you because no one can love you the way I can. Not even perfect Drew."

Her mouth made a little o. It took all his willpower not to move in and capture her lips, kiss her hard and deep, forcing her to confront her true feelings. Instead, he fisted his own hands and stayed still.

A broken sigh escaped her. Confusion along with a longing she couldn't hide flashed in her gaze. "I'm trying to figure some stuff out. But it's not what you think with Drew and me."

Hope surged. He searched her gaze, falling into the ocean blue depths that emanated a swirl of emotions. "Tell me."

The command was simple, and she seemed to realize he was here to truly listen, not judge her for pursuing another man. God knows, he'd broken something between them, and he wasn't stupid enough to assume she'd wait for him to return. He had no rights here. Pretending he did disrespected them both, even though his insides roared with pain at the idea of her being intimate with Drew.

"I was his date for a finance dinner with his employees. The night was a bit…awkward. I didn't really fit in with his crowd, but Drew didn't seem to notice. He wanted to get more serious. I realized we weren't a good fit, so I broke up with him."

"And the kiss?"

"There was paparazzi waiting when we came out. He took the opportunity to kiss me in front of the cameras as proof he was serious about our relationship. I wasn't pleased."

The tightness in his chest eased. She'd broken up with him. She'd recognized, on her own, he was rotten on the inside, and a dizzying relief poured through Owen. "He tried to pretend you were still together. That you had an ongoing sexual relationship."

Her jaw tightened, and temper snapped in her eyes. "We never had sex. Not that it's your business," she added.

He tried desperately to keep from giving a primitive, manlike yell of satisfaction, choosing to just nod. "I know."

"Drew asked about you, and I told him about our past. He didn't accept the breakup—told me he'd give me some space to rethink things. He probably thought sending the flowers would make you back off. Along with coming to challenge you like some ridiculous cock fight. What a jerk."

"Classic territorial move," Owen said, the final pieces fitting together. Again, he couldn't blame the guy for trying to hold on to Chloe, but lying wasn't the way to her heart. The real challenge was to crack open her defenses and allow her not only to love him but trust him again. "So here we are."

A broken laugh escaped her lips. "Guess so. Vivian knows, and so does the staff. We'll just have to ride out the press for a little while until a new juicy story takes my place. Dad called to remind me about Evie's birthday. Mia invited us to the farm this weekend so it will be a good escape."

"Harper called me, too. Asked me to join them."

She jerked back. "I—I didn't know. It may not be a good idea for us to be there together. Not now."

He placed the beer down on the side table and reached over. Her head tilted back to stare at him with wariness, but he smiled gently, his hand pushing back the wayward strand of hair covering her brow. "I disagree. I think it's a great idea. We both need to get away and spend some quiet time together. I won't push, Chloe. I just want the opportunity to talk. Ride horses. Visit with the Bishops. I miss you."

She sucked in a breath, but not before he caught the gleam of longing in her eyes. "I don't like the feelings I have around you," she finally said.

God, he loved her directness, the fire trapped within her kind heart.

"I'm sure you don't. It's easier to hate me and run away. But this is too important to ignore and you're too damn brave to back away from a mess. Even when you're scared."

Her body trembled. "You used to be my best friend," she whispered. "But now I don't know what we are to each other."

Owen broke. Muttering a curse, he reached for her, tucking her against his chest and holding tight. Her shoulders trembled, and he stroked her hair, giving her the comfort she so desperately needed. He held her for a long time, treasuring the firm warmth of her body, her fresh scent, the way she clung back, accepting his embrace.

"Come to the farm with me, Chloe," he said, pressing a kiss to the top of her head. "Give us some time to figure it out together."

Her voice was muffled against his chest. "I don't want to pretend we can go back. We're not the same young kids we were years ago."

"No, we're not. But maybe we can revisit the beginning so we can find a new ending for us. I want that chance."

She waited a while to answer. They held each other as the seconds ticked by, and Owen wished time would stop. Her closeness completed an empty piece of him he'd been mourning since he walked away. He held his breath as she slowly broke the embrace and took a few steps back.

"Okay. We'll go to the farm."

He smiled at her. Her wobbly smile back touched his heart.

He left her place with a fresh hope and looked forward to the weekend.

* * * *

The Robin's Nest B&B was nestled in the quirky upstate town of Gardiner, which held twisty country roads and a charming array of farm markets, shops, and cafés, all framed by the mighty Shawangunk mountains. Endless green acres sprawled out for miles, the red barns for the horses dotted in a long line from the distance behind a pretty white fence. As Chloe got out of the car with Dad and Alyssa, a light-hearted joy flowed through her, reminding her this was where it had all begun.

Her love for animal rescue. Her blossoming into a woman rather than an angry girl. Forgiving her father for the past and moving forward. Getting her own horse to care for and love. Falling in love for the first time.

But most of all, it was a reminder that family was everything.

"Is it okay if I go to the stables?" she asked.

Her father laughed. "Sure—I'll bring in your luggage and meet you there in a bit."

"Thanks!" She took off at a run, flying down the familiar path that wove through the woods, then exploded into a clearing where horses grazed and the mountain's jagged, earth-colored rocks rose before her like a king on his throne. She spotted Harper and Aidan immediately, washing down two of the horses, playfully squirting water at each other.

"Chloe, you're here!" Harper said, dropping the hose and coming to greet her. "You look amazing!"

They hugged and Aidan walked over, a big grin slashing across his sun-creased face. The Irish horse trainer had come to the farm to help train Phoenix, an abused rescued horse, to win the Triple Crown. Phoenix had fallen short but captured America's heart and everyone else's along his journey.

And Aidan had captured Harper's. They'd gotten married and doubled the size of the horse rescue farm.

"We missed you around here," Aidan said, jerking his head toward the stables. "Especially Chloe's Pride."

"I know, it's been so damn busy with the Spagarelli case at work along with other issues. I promise to get here more often."

"No worries, she's well taken care of," Harper said with a wink. "Seems she's got a crush on our new stud Maui."

Chloe laughed. "Maybe Owen can test him out when he gets here. See if he's worthy of my horse."

Aidan cocked his head. "Things okay with you two? We didn't know, but Mia really wanted all of you here for the party."

The Bishops had all watched Chloe and Owen fall in love and pursue a serious relationship during college. They'd also comforted her when it had all broken apart, but Chloe had always been careful never to badmouth Owen to the clan. He was part of them, and she never wanted to come between them. "He's back to stay in New York and we've been working this abuse case together. Finally have a date for a civil trial. We're going to see how things unfold."

Harper nodded. "We love you both and just want to see you happy, however that unfolds."

"Thanks. Now, what should I get to work on?"

Aidan waved his hand in the air. "Nope, not this weekend. We've got plenty of helpers now, and we want you to enjoy yourself. There's a cupcake festival this weekend you may want to hit. Have you seen Mia or Ethan yet?"

"No, Dad and Alyssa went ahead to the inn. I'm going to check on Chloe's Pride and then head back."

"Sounds good."

She strolled down to Barn C, enjoying the musty scents and the hay beneath her feet. She grabbed an apple, reached the stall, and whistled low, putting her hand out. The beautiful white horse did a double take of recognition, then immediately pushed out her nuzzle for affection. Chloe crooned love words to the horse, slowly feeding her the apple.

Horses had been the gateway to her passion. The magnificent creatures were so full of love to give, yet too many discarded them as worthless once they couldn't race, or work, or do something equally useful.

Chloe had learned early on that love was the most useful element of all.

She spent some time in the barn, showering the horse with affection and slowly felt the air rise and charge around her.

She turned. Owen stood framed in the doorway, watching. His long legs were spread apart, hands fisted at his hips, gaze locked on hers. He wore faded jeans and a simple black T-shirt that stretched across his broad chest. His hair curled messily across his brow, reminding her of when he was young.

Since she'd agreed to come to the farm, he'd given her space, spending most of his time out at site visits or the courthouse. Seeing him in his element made a shiver race down her spine and slowly spread, warming her body more than the muggy heat.

"I knew you'd come to the barn first," he said, his lips quirking in a hint of a smile. "How's your girl doing?"

Chloe's Pride let out a whinny, sensing more company to demand affection from.

They laughed. "Thriving, but I heard she missed me. Have to get out here more. Plus, when I do ride, it's like the world makes better sense around me."

"I know exactly what you mean," he said. "I just peeked in on Flower and promised her some exercise this weekend. Want to check in at the house and then ride?"

"Sounds good."

She followed him out of the barn, but suddenly he stopped short, jerking back and almost sending her stumbling. "Ah, crap, he did it again! Scared the hell out of me."

Chloe peeked around and there he was, blocking their path.

Hei-Hei.

The giant Polish chicken looked monstrous up close, with heavy, fat jowls, beady eyes, and a bunch of crazy white feathers sticking out of his head like a crown. The chicken let out a shriek at the sight of Owen and began clawing the ground madly with his hooked feet. Owen made a low noise of distress, and Chloe bit back a giggle.

Owen and Hei-Hei had a complicated relationship.

"Get away from me, you crazy chicken," Owen commanded, trying to intimidate the creature by pulling himself to full height.

"Umm, Owen, I don't think you should—"

"I won't let him intimidate me any longer!"

"But—"

The chicken cocked his head, considering the command.

Then charged.

Owen let out a low yell and Hei-Hei began pecking at his feet, moving his body side to side in some type of bizarre dance. Chloe tried to stop it, but Owen seemed to want to protect her, even though she'd always been able to control the chicken. Hei-Hei only listened to Chloe, Ethan, and of course, Mia.

Suddenly, a female voice whipped out and echoed in the air. "Hei-Hei! How dare you treat Owen like that—he's a friend." The chicken stopped his insane pecking and regarded his mistress. Mia wagged a finger at him in warning. "I mean it. Now go back to the house and if you don't behave, I'll let Evie play with you again."

Hei-Hei rushed away from Owen and began rubbing his feathers against Mia's legs, as if begging her to reconsider the punishment. Chloe imagined playing with a one-year-old wasn't high on the chicken's list of fun things. "I don't know why he's always been so naughty with you, Owen," Mia said, shaking his head. "He must've snuck past me in the commotion back at the house."

Owen cleared his throat. "No problem. I was handling it okay."

Chloe bit back the giggle that threatened and headed over to Mia. "Hei-Hei just likes to make a dramatic entrance," Chloe said with a grin, giving her honorable aunt a huge hug. "Sorry we got caught up with the horses."

"You both always do. And each other."

Heat flushed her cheeks, but Chloe ignored the comment. Mia practically glowed with health and happiness. Her trim figure was fashionably dressed in linen shorts, a lacy white blouse, and white sandals. Dark hair curled under her chin in a blunt, stylish cut. Her amber eyes gazed back with her usual frankness, boldly studying the two of them to decipher exactly what was going on. Chloe knew she'd be grilled by everyone the moment they got her in private. Mia might be the owner of one of the most successful PR firms that handled her father's campaigns, but underneath, the woman still adored good gossip.

"I cannot believe we're celebrating Evie's first birthday," Chloe said, grabbing Mia's hands. "How did a year go by so fast?"

"With little sleep," Mia quipped, squeezing her hands. "But worth every moment. Ophelia's making dinner for everyone tomorrow night with a cake to celebrate. Why don't we grab a bite to eat first and then you can take an early evening ride? We put out some sandwiches and ordered pizzas."

"Sounds great—I'm starving," Owen said.

Mia laughed. "Harper said when you first started your volunteer work, all you cared about was your phone and next meal."

He winced. "I outgrew one out of two. I'd give up my phone any day."

They laughed and walked to the main inn where everyone waited. Ophelia and Kyle welcomed them warmly, and Chloe noticed Ophelia had not only ordered a variety of pizzas, but created a tray of sandwiches and wraps, with a Greek salad and crusty rolls of bread. She remembered eating dinner here that first night and being overwhelmed at the amount of delicious food Ophelia happily cooked. As the main owners of the B&B, the married couple had turned the inn into a highly successful retreat that was consistently booked all year round. With her long golden hair, willowy body, and blue eyes, Ophelia reminded her of a fairytale princess. They all fell into easy chatter, but Chloe noticed her father refused to acknowledge Owen's presence. Alyssa kept shooting him pointed looks, but every time Owen tried to say hello, her father became engaged in another conversation.

Great. The governor of New York was acting like a toddler.

"Ah, there's our guest of honor," Mia said. "Did she wake up early?"

Chloe turned to see Ethan and his daughter, Evie, walk through the door. The baby had a head full of auburn hair, amber eyes, and a stubborn jaw just like her mama. Her chunky legs kicked with glee at the crowd of people, pegging her as an extrovert. She wore pink stretchy leggings, a glittery shirt with a unicorn on it, and pink walking shoes.

Ethan laughed and chucked Evie under the chin. "Her naps are getting shorter each day. She tried to crawl after Hei-Hei but he was too fast for her."

"Good, that chicken needed a good punishment," Owen muttered.

Ethan called out greetings to everyone, and Chloe ran over. Her heart melted as Ethan handed her the baby, leaning in to kiss Chloe on the cheek. "Good to see you, Chlo," he said, those kind eyes full of warmth. "We missed you."

"Missed you more," she said, cooing and tickling the baby, relishing her shrieky, happy giggles. Ethan had been the one to guide her through her freshman year of college, when she felt aimless, angry, and full of pain. Recognizing a fellow wounded soul, he showed her how the animals could heal, and ended up changing her life. She loved him like a second father, and they consistently corresponded via text on a regular basis. With his rugged, quiet aura, russet hair, and gentle touch, he'd retired from the military after a terrible injury and came back to work on the farm. His ability to heal Phoenix helped turn the horse into a racing legend.

Evie happily became the center of attention as everyone took their turns with her. Chloe noticed Owen block her father to the side and say a few words. Holding her breath, she watched as Dad's face tightened. Then he gave a sharp nod and marched outside.

Owen followed.

Chloe met Alyssa's supportive gaze and hoped for the best.

Chapter Eleven

"Sir, can we speak frankly?"

Owen ignored his rapidly beating heart and faced the man who'd been the first to capture Chloe's heart. Jonathan Lake was an intimidating man, from his steely gaze, muscled frame, and powerful energy that beat in waves around his figure. Owen had always been a bit scared of him, agreeing with his view that Owen would never be good enough for Chloe. But now, it was time to set the past straight and tell his truths.

If he wanted a fresh start with Chloe, he needed to begin with her father.

"Frankly is the only way I speak," Jonathan said, leaning against the rail of the porch. "Why don't you tell me what's on your mind?"

"Chloe. I'm not sure what she's told you about us yet, but I specifically came back for her. To make things right. To get a second chance. I have no intention of hurting her."

Jonathan lifted a brow. "You already did. Enough that I had to watch my daughter in pain for a very long time. It took her a while to put the pieces back together. So let me tell you my intentions, Owen Salt. You are going to leave her alone so she can get on with her life."

He got a front row seat to how a competitor felt in direct opposition to the governor. The man was razor sharp, focused and intent on tearing Owen apart. This time, though, he knew who he was and what he wanted. Owen kept his position, meeting the man's eyes in a direct, calm gaze.

"That's not going to happen, sir. I'm here to stay. I'm not sure if Chloe will ever allow me a second chance, but I'm not giving up. I'm not the same man who left four years ago, but I've never stopped loving her.

Not one damn day."

Jonathan began to pace, his hands reflexively squeezing into fists. Owen recognized the same exact habit Chloe always demonstrated. He wished he had a stress ball to throw the man. "If you loved her, why'd you leave? I could have gotten you a damn job right here in New York— you never had to go to California. You left because you wanted to, and it's time you admit it."

The memory of his fateful decision still had the power to rip him apart. Remembering her face when he refused to respond after her begging him to stay. The splinter of raw vulnerability and pain when she realized he was breaking up with her. "No. I left because I had to. I'm not sure if you can understand the position I was in. Chloe always had a clear direction of what she wanted to accomplish. I was lost. Do you have any idea how difficult it was knowing I could've been in some cushy job with your help or my grandfather's by just asking, and choosing to go out on my own instead? The only identity I had as a man was loving your daughter. Is that what you'd really want for her?"

Jonathan practically growled at him. "No. That's exactly why I never thought you were good for her!"

"You can't help who you love. I fell for Chloe the second I laid eyes on her. Do you think that was easy? Being a nineteen-year-old kid and knowing your fate was right there, but you had to figure shit out first in order to be worthy of it? Have you ever experienced anything like that?"

"Yes—with Chloe's mother. But I stayed and made it work. We figured it out together."

Owen shook his head with frustration. "I couldn't. When I lost my grandfather, I spun out. I didn't want to be reliant on anyone but myself. And my gut sensed I'd end up losing Chloe anyway, maybe hurting her more and taking her down with me. I can't change the past, I can only tell you I grew up. I know who I am, and that I'm worthy of your daughter. And with or without your permission, I'm going to try and convince her to give me another chance."

Jonathan blew out a breath and halted mid-stride, facing him. "I liked Drew."

Owen refused to flinch under the insult. "He's not right for her. He's more smitten with the idea of Chloe rather than her core. In fact, I think he's more into having you as his future father-in-law."

Jonathan let out a short laugh. "He did text me a lot."

Owen grinned. "He sent her a lot of roses."

The man wrinkled his nose. "She hates those."

"I know," he said softly. "I'm sorry I couldn't be what she needed before, but I am now. I'm just asking for you to give me a chance, too."

Jonathan rubbed his head and swore under his breath. "Fine. I'll back off and let you both work it out. If you hurt her again, I won't let you get away this time. I'll find you."

The threat by any other man would have sounded empty and like a wanna-be mobster.

From Jonathon's mouth, Owen knew it was fact.

"I won't. I can only hope to gain your respect along the way. Thanks for listening." Owen turned toward the door, but the man's voice stopped him cold.

"I respect you made some hard choices and owned up to them," he said grudgingly. "Most men I know are full of empty excuses. Your grandfather would be proud of that, Owen."

Emotion constricted his chest. "Thanks."

He went back inside. Chloe sent him an anxious glance, and he smiled, giving her a nod.

The relief and happiness flickering on her face gave him hope. She wanted him to be on good terms with her father. It meant she saw a future for them. It might be misty now, but Owen intended to make it clearer with every day that passed.

* * * *

The sun sank over the horizon and the mountains shimmered in a haze of muted pinks and oranges. The horses' hooves thundered over the pasture, caught in the rush of an old-fashioned race. Owen leaned forward to urge Flower on, but Chloe had always been a better rider. She guided Chloe's Pride to the lead, her black hair blowing in the wind, her laugh rising in the air and caressing his ears.

She passed the marker first and gave a wild whoop, and he grinned as he eased back on the reins, watching her perfect mount on the white horse, who twitched her tail with pride at the win.

God, she was beautiful. This was the woman he remembered—a free spirit tearing around the farm in her zeal to do her best for the animals, morphing into a goddess as she rode on the back of her horse without fear, open to the unknown path ahead.

And he knew in his heart, no matter how far he ran, no matter how hard he tried to forget, he'd always be the man who was helplessly, foolishly in love with this woman.

"Got a bit rusty there in surfer city, huh?" she teased, trotting Chloe's Pride over.

He patted Flower. "Just taking it easy on you girls. Didn't want to push you too hard."

She rolled her eyes. "Oh, please, I've won every race we ever had and you know it."

"Only because I like watching you from the back. You have a fine…form."

He relished the spot of color on her cheeks. "Chauvinist," she muttered, tugging the horse toward the trail. "Let's go to the creek."

The rocky path twisted and turned through the woods. The sound of rushing water mixed with the chirp of birds and rustle of leaves. The dying rays of sun cast trickles of rainbow light through the thick shade of trees. They picked their way to the bottom, then tied up the horses at the creek where they could grab a drink. Settling on two massive rocks, they sat together in silence, breathing in the stillness and life of the woods around them. The musky scents of earth saturated the air, mixing with Chloe's unique smell of wildflowers, making him a bit woozy.

"Are you going to tell me what happened with Dad?" she asked, propping her hands behind her back.

"We came to an understanding. I told him I was working hard to see if we can have a second chance together. He had some questions for me."

A laugh rose from her lips. "I bet he did. How did you both leave it?"

"He's not going to put a hit out on me. Yet."

"Dad gets a bit intense."

"I remember. But it's because he loves you. I can deal with that."

He reached out and took her hand and she let him. Owen soaked up the warmth of her presence, the slide of her fingers in his, the feeling of finally being home. At the farm.

With her.

"You know the hardest part about you leaving me?" she asked.

He looked over, but she was staring out at the water. He studied her profile, the strong chin, the pert shape of her nose, the smooth skin and fall of her dark hair. "What?"

"I didn't know how to trust myself anymore. I always believed in my gut we'd be together forever. I know that may be naïve, especially since we were so young. But it was like the only thing in my life I didn't doubt.

Maybe that was wrong. Maybe I pushed you for too much, too soon."

"I always wanted everything you did, Chloe. I just wasn't able to give it to you. But I'm here, and now I can. If you open up a little to the possibilities."

She turned her head and their gazes met, connected, melded. The air peaked with sensual tension, and he remembered the first time they'd made love, a blanket spread out in the pasture, under a sky full of stars.

"You want to go to the cupcake festival with me?" she finally said.

He smiled and squeezed her hand. "I'd love to."

"Then it's a date. But we better head back—it'll be dark soon."

He helped her up from the rock and they got back on the horses.

This time, they rode side by side the whole time.

Chapter Twelve

The festival was held in the back fields behind Wrights Farm. Endless booths lined up filled with various vendors, selling homemade cupcakes, treats, food, and crafts. Music drifted from a tent with the live band, and local breweries offered samples of beer and wine tastings. Dogs walked happily along on leashes, and the pet bakery sold dozens of specialty treats for happy canines.

Ophelia, Kyle, Harper, and Aidan had stayed back to watch Evie, insisting that Mia and Ethan get some time to themselves. They all drove together, while Owen blasted his favorite playlist of alternative music, to both Chloe's and Ethan's delight. Mia just groaned and talked about the terrible names such as Cold War Kids, Cage the Elephant, and Portugal the Man, but she was drowned out by all the singing.

After they parked and made their way to the entrance, Chloe asked to see his playlists. "You had all the best songs," she said. "I'm terrible at organizing stuff on my phone, can I take a look?"

"Sure, the code is 1212."

Chloe chuckled and opened up the app. "Maybe you should think of getting a smarter password," she teased.

"You're probably right. But there's so damn many of them, I want it easy. The one I always replay is at the top—oh, crap, wait! Umm, can I have my phone back really quick?"

"Sure, but it's right here, under…" She trailed off, staring at the screen. "Songs for Chloe?"

She glanced up. His normally ruddy cheeks were red stained, and pure embarrassment flickered from his pale blue eyes. It took her a few moments for the realization to hit, and then she confirmed by quickly ticking off all the songs listed.

Songs she loved. Songs they'd listened to over and over. Songs they'd fallen in love with together. A playlist for her.

The last song was Etta James, *At Last*.

He cleared his throat and snatched the phone back. "Umm, yeah. I kind of made up a list of my favorites, and they happen to be yours, too."

A wave of heat washed over her, having nothing to do with the sun. "Owen, you made me a mix tape."

He stared at her in a bit of confusion. "I just made a place to go when I missed you."

Her legs got weak just like the trope, and for one crazy moment, she almost jumped into his arms and kissed him.

"Ready, guys?" Mia asked, turning to see where they were.

Owen shoved the phone in his pocket and fumbled out money for the tickets. Delight and joy unfurled inside her at the evidence. He hadn't forgotten her, after all. In a way, he'd taken her with him.

Chloe laughed as Ethan wrapped his wife tight and smacked a noisy kiss on her lips. "This was our first date, princess."

"I remember," Chloe interrupted. "You dragged me with you to play chaperone, pretending to hate each other, but I knew it was backed-up sexual tension."

"What do you think, horse man?" Mia teased, tilting her head up toward her husband. "Should we go eat cupcakes?"

"Absolutely. We'll revisit the first time you fell in love with me years ago."

Mia sputtered. "Excuse me? If you recall, I thought you were an overbearing jerk when you forced me to accompany you to the festival."

Ethan puffed up with male pride. "Until I found your perfect cupcake and fed it to you. You were all sweetness and sugar after that. You fell hard. Oww."

He rubbed his arm where she'd punched him. Chloe let out a laugh and they agreed to meet back in an hour so they could explore. Mia was already darting toward the specialty cupcakes, looking like a kid spotting a new bike on Christmas morning.

"Ready to eat, babe?"

His voice was a low whisper near her ear, the endearment making her tummy dip. She turned slightly and found his pale blue gaze pinned to her mouth. Her tongue flicked out to wet her lower lips, and a mischievous grin tugged the edge of his lip. Now she was the one with hot cheeks while shivers bumped down her spine. He was so damn sexy with that goatee and boy next door face, but especially because the world seemed to fall away when they were together. His razor-sharp focus was all for her.

On pure impulse, she raised up on tiptoes and pressed her mouth against his firm, warm lips.

"Let's do it."

They held hands and enjoyed the festival. He remembered her love for Cookie Monster and bought her a bright blue cupcake, feeding it to her in tiny bites as they strolled. They sipped local sample of ciders and beer, bought a pot of honey for Ophelia's kitchen, and snatched up a homemade rum cake for them to eat later in the weekend. Children screamed from the bouncy tent, balloons were held tight, bobbing in the air, and it was as if time had stopped, freezing them in a memory from the past.

But it wasn't, because they weren't kids any longer. As she darted in and out of the stalls, and Owen stood on the sideline watching, smiling at her, Chloe realized things weren't the same. The man beside her still held the childlike wonder she always admired but it was now tempered with a maturity and confidence. He used to chase after her, as if trying to keep up to make her happy, but now it was as if he held his own presence, able to stay silent and watch. He'd grown into himself.

They'd begun to circle back when her gaze caught on a young woman with a boy sitting beside a sign that said *Puppies for Sale*. There was a crowd of kids leaning over and poking at a box. Owen's hand tightened on hers as he led her over.

The worn box held a tiny black puppy. Soft whines emitted from its throat, and Chloe watched the furball try to escape the mass of frantic hands trying to grab a touch. She quickly diagnosed a problem with the puppy's right front leg. It held an awkward gait as the pup tried to run back and forth in the box. "Only fifty bucks for a new puppy!" the young woman announced. "Would make a wonderful new friend."

Parents called their kids back, leaving Owen and Chloe. "Is something wrong with him?" Chloe asked. "He's walking funny."

The woman waved a hand in the air and laughed. "Just hurt his paw a few minutes ago, but he's fine. No issues. Runt of the litter so you get a discount. I normally charge a hundred."

Immediately, Owen's face closed up. "Did you manage to sell the others?" he asked tightly.

"Sure did. This male is the last one left, and I have to sell it today."

Owen's voice iced up. "Why? What will happen to him if you don't?"

The young boy beside her turned a haunted gaze up to them. "Mama said we have to get rid of it either way," he said. "Puppies are expensive."

The young woman ignored the boy. "I'll drop it off at a shelter," she said curtly.

Chloe knew immediately she was lying. It was in her eyes, and the truth hit her full force. If the puppy didn't sell, she'd dump him somewhere and leave the pup to fend for himself. With a lame leg, the pup wouldn't have a chance. Chloe doubted anyone here would buy an obviously injured puppy for that type of money.

Once again, an animal was looked on as an object rather than a living creature who not only wanted to live, but to be loved. She'd seen it a thousand times before. Overbred dogs produced puppies. Puppies were sold for the profit, and whatever dog didn't sell got dumped.

Rage overtook her, but she bit it back. The helplessness was the worst—knowing this woman would probably do it again, and never think twice about the repercussions of the murders trailed behind her.

Her thoughts whirled with ideas of how to handle the situation until Owen spoke.

"I'll take him."

The woman lit up. "Great! Let me just—oh, can you wait a moment? I have to take this call, Sam will help. We have change if you need it. Make sure you count the money," she counseled the boy, turning away and hitting the button for the call.

Shocked, Chloe watched Owen kneel in front of the boy. The kid wore ripped shorts, an old Mets baseball jersey, and a dirty blue hat. His face was a bit gaunt, his dark eyes sad and solemn as he stared back. "Sam, my name is Owen. Do you have one dog that births all the puppies? Or many?"

"Just one. She's old, though, and Mama said she may not be able to have any more litters. I wanted to keep one but I can't. Mama said we need to sell them."

"I understand. Does anyone ever hurt the puppies?"

The boy shook his head hard. "No, but this one was super little and jumped out and hurt his leg. Now he don't walk good. But I'm glad you're taking him 'cause I don't want him to go into the woods like the other ones. I'm afraid he'd get cold."

A sob trapped in her throat, Chloe kept still and listened. "Okay, listen to me, Sam, this is important. I'm going to give you my card. If your dog has anymore puppies, or your mom gets another dog that keeps having puppies, I want you to call me. You see, baby animals need a lot of extra care and I can find good homes for all of them."

"You mean even the sick ones don't have to go to the woods?"

"That's right. I'll take care of the sick ones too. Are you able to use the phone on your own?"

The boy puffed up. "Sure, I'm seven already! I have a phone to do video games on but I know how to make a call."

"Good. Take this card and put it someplace safe. I'd like it to be our secret, but I understand if you need to tell your mom. I don't want you to get in trouble."

The boy nodded. "Okay, but I don't need to tell Mama everything. I don't think she likes the puppies like I do, anyway."

"I don't think so either. When you grow up, you'll take care of your animals, right? They depend on us to treat them good and then they love us forever."

"I promise."

Owen gave him the card and Sam tucked it in his pocket. Then he took out fifty dollars and pressed it into the boy's hands.

The woman rushed back, a big smile on her face. "All set?"

"Yes." Owen didn't thank her. Just nodded at Sam and scooped the puppy gently out of the box, cradling it against his broad chest. "Bye, Sam."

"Bye, mister."

They walked a few feet away and watched until the woman packed up and left with the boy. The puppy mewed in distress, pressing against Owen, who stroked his head with gentle fingers and murmured soothing phrases. His face reflected a fierce focus toward the vulnerable animal, a man intent on righting a wrong, a warrior and protector rolled into one. Like his grandfather.

And Chloe realized she still loved Owen Salt.

Maybe she'd never stopped.

"I think I just got myself a puppy," he slowly said, looking at her with slight shock. "I wasn't sure what to do, but I couldn't let her take him back."

"Neither could I." She leaned in, creating a tight circle. "You were amazing, especially with Sam. We really had no other choice, did we?"

He sighed. "No. Let's go introduce our new addition to the rest of the family and get a vet to look at that leg." He shook his head. "But damn, he's a cute one. And special. I can feel it."

She stared at Owen, torn between hysterical laughter and tears as the walls she'd carefully built to keep him away crashed down around her. "Yes, he certainly is."

They walked toward Mia and Ethan, and Chloe wondered why she already felt like they were a family.

Chapter Thirteen

"I can't take the cuteness," Harper said, watching the puppy toddle around the blanket, peering up at them. "Ophelia, please can't we take him inside?"

"No. I've told you over and over, Harper, no animals in the inn. Guests can be allergic and dog hair gets everywhere. You know the rules."

Owen swallowed a laugh as Harper gave a pissy grunt, eliciting Aidan to laugh and tug playfully at her hair. "*Mo gra'* you'll have all night to cuddle with him. Did you settle on a name yet, Owen?"

Harper had already volunteered to take the puppy overnight so Owen and Chloe could sleep at the inn. Jonathan and Alyssa were staying with Mia and Ehtan. Owen knew the pup would be in perfect hands.

"No. Figured Chloe can give me a hand with such an important task."

"It has to be a Disney name, of course," Chloe said. "To stay with tradition."

All of the rescue animals at the Bishop farm were dubbed with names from Disney characters they all loved. They took the naming seriously, knowing once an animal received a name, the new identity represented a chance at a new life of happiness and care.

And a rebuilding of trust.

Harper had gone into full rescue mode and after a thorough vet visit, found the puppy had carpal hyperextension syndrome, caused by poor muscle tone. The condition was common in certain puppies. Thank God, it was nothing serious and would eventually heal on its own—the idea that a perfectly healthy puppy would've been dumped without thought burned through him, but he had to make peace with it or he'd explode.

It was something he'd learned well in animal law. So he rescued the ones he could, and that made a difference.

It had to be enough.

He felt a hand on his shoulder and glanced up. Chloe gave him a smile, and he realized she sensed his thoughts and distress. She'd always been completely in tune with his emotions, a woman who truly understood him from the inside out. He gave a small nod in thanks, took a breath, and stood.

"I'll get him settled in the barn while we eat," he said.

"The birthday girl is going to freak if she sees him," Ethan said, glancing toward the porch where Mia was playing with Evie. "Better keep him hidden or it will be like playing with Hei-Hei all over again."

"Oh, stop, she's an angel with the animals," Harper said. "She's just fascinated with the chicken's head feathers."

"Personally, I'm glad Hei-Hei found his match," Owen announced. "Let him be the one running away and terrified."

Aidan arched a brow. "Still have issues with him, Owen? One day, you two will need to form a truce."

"Only truce we'll ever have is when he's on the table for dinner."

"Owen!" Chloe gasped. "That's terrible."

"Just kidding, babe. Meet you inside."

Laughter scattered behind him. He realized he'd used the familiar endearment without thought, but somehow, it felt right. Today, they'd made progress. The farm was definitely helping strip back the layers so they could re-discover each other all over again.

He set the puppy up in a small crate, next to the horses in the barn for company. The black furball settled right in to sleep, exhausted by the stressful day. He gave Flower and Bambi a stroke on the nose and fed them a carrot. "Keep watch on him, okay? I'll be back."

When he got back to the inn, everyone had gathered in the dining room for the party. The guest of honor wore a red sparkly party dress, red Dorothy-like shoes, and a birthday crown. Her highchair was decorated with balloons and wavy sparkly flags that fascinated Evie. She waved her chubby fingers, watching them float and fly in delight.

The table was filled with all the comfort foods he loved. Salted, maple cured ham sat amidst cut apples and bacon, and endless side dishes of mashed potatoes, biscuits, vegetable quiches, and creamed spinach. He ate heartily, relaxing into the familiar banter of the family, a twist of compliments amidst good-natured teasing and insults between the men. Kyle's father, Patrick, was at the other head of the table, grunting now and then, but basically concentrating on his full plate. Jonathan held his own, even when Ethan pushed at his politics, and Mia hotly defended her PR client against her husband, to everyone's amusement.

He watched Chloe shine amidst the people she loved, her face open and happy, her laughter loud and quick. Longing washed over him with a mind-blowing intensity. God, he wanted this with her. To be her lover and husband, part of this amazing clan who gathered for celebrations and held each other up during the hard times. He finally wanted forever, and he had to believe it wasn't too late.

They all helped clear the table and clean up. Mia brought in the cake decorated in bright unicorn colors, topped with one candle. She snapped endless pictures of Evie's wonder at the colorful creation before her. They sang Happy Birthday, and the toddler dove in hard to her first piece of cake, smushing it over her mouth and fingers while she screamed with happiness.

"I brought champagne," Chloe said, corking open the bottle and grabbing glasses and pouring generously.

"None for me," Ophelia said with a smile.

Kyle blinked. "You love champagne. Come on, sweetheart, there's no guests to worry about tomorrow. We cleared this weekend months ago."

"None for me either," Mia said.

Chloe gave a sigh. "Really, guys? I thought we'd get a bit giddy tonight. Stay up late watching Disney movies, right?"

Jonathan groaned. "Who needs a Disney movie? Every time I step on the farm I feel like I'm dragged into one."

Mia laughed. "It's okay, Jonathan. I always loved your grumpy side. It's why we work so well together."

"Come on, Dad. If you watched more movies, you could help us name the new pup. You need more information."

Alyssa grinned and touched her husband's shoulder. "I think your father is better suited to political thrillers."

"Definitely. The only movie that sticks out is Cinderella—something about the glass slipper and Fairy Godmother, I guess. Oh, and that fat mouse with the T-shirt!"

"Gus-Gus?" Chloe asked.

Jonathan shrugged. "I guess, I don't know the name. I liked him. He was funny, loyal, and kind of a misfit."

Immediately, Owen met Chloe's gaze.

"Gus-Gus," they said together, as if lightning had just struck them both.

"Dad, you did it! What a perfect name for the puppy!"

"Agreed," Owen said, watching Jonathan's shocked face.

"Yeah? You like it?" he grumbled, trying to act cool.

"We love it," Chloe reassured him.

"I'm proud of you, honey," Alyssa said, shooting Chloe and Owen a wink from across the table.

Jonathan puffed up and nodded. "Yeah, it's definitely a great name."

They were just making arrangements to open up Evie's gifts in the living room when Ophelia spoke. "Actually, I wanted to make an announcement tonight. It's a cause for champagne."

"Then why aren't you drinking it, Tink?" Ethan joked.

A flush suffused her face. She glanced at Kyle, and suddenly, Kyle's father slammed his hand down on the table. "Holy shit, she's pregnant!"

Everyone whirled around to stare at Patrick, then Ophelia.

Ophelia burst into laughter, blue eyes sparkling. "Well, thank you, Patrick, for helping me out here. Yes, I'm pregnant!"

Owen watched Kyle's face change from shock, to surprise, then finally, pure delight. "A baby?" he whispered, cupping her cheeks with a trembling hand. "We're going to have a baby?"

"Yes. We're going to have a baby," Ophelia said, pressing a kiss to his lips.

"So am I."

Owen shook his head, his brain about to explode. He looked at Mia, who'd made the announcement, and Ethan jerked back, staring at his wife. "What did you say?"

Mia jumped up and down in her seat. "I'm pregnant, too! We're going to have babies together!"

The table exploded and Evie bounced in her highchair, echoing her mother's moves. Hugs and kisses and congratulations went around. Chloe distributed the rest of the champagne and called for a toast, replacing Mia's and Ophelia's with sparkling cider.

Aidan glanced suspiciously at Harper when she didn't grasp the glass immediately.

Everyone fell silent.

Harper rolled her eyes. "Hell, no, not even close. I'll take the bottle, please."

They laughed and toasted while Evie threw the rest of her cake in the air.

And Owen watched Chloe, his heart full, knowing it had been a perfect day.

* * * *

Chloe stared at the floral papered wall that was the only barrier to Owen.

Sighing, she glanced around the familiar room. She'd spent an entire summer here, mandated to community service, stuck with Mia, who'd been a stranger, estranged from her father as she tried desperately to process her mother's death and all the feelings that came with it.

She'd healed here. It had been the beginning of a second chance for her.

Today, she realized she wanted that with Owen.

Even though she was still scared. Scared to re-open herself to that type of emotion, especially knowing how deeply he had the power to hurt her. He swore he was ready for a full commitment now, but there were never guarantees. Another job opportunity could lure him away. He could get bored with the pressured lifestyle of being in the public scrutiny twenty-four-seven. He could fall out of love with her.

Yet, she'd been taught by all those people at the dinner table love was worth the risk. It had to be her choice this time. She knew Owen would never come to her. Chloe believed it would have taken months to build up to taking a leap, but right now, in this moment, her heart craved only one thing to fulfill the empty, aching need inside.

Him.

She glanced in the mirror. Boxer shorts. A worn V-neck T-shirt. Definitely not an outfit for seduction, but Chloe knew the stakes were bigger than sexy lingerie or carefully crafted words. This needed to be stripped to the bone raw, and hell if she'd try to hide behind surface appearances.

She tiptoed down the hall, paused in front of his door, and turned the knob.

It opened soundlessly. She stepped into the dark room.

"I hoped you'd come."

He was sitting on the edge of the bed. Bare-chested. A pair of low-slung pants clung to his hips. Blonde hair tousled and wild, falling over his brow. Even within the shadows, the heat in his pale blue gaze was like twin laser beams, drilling deep to the core.

Heart hammering in her chest, she walked toward him. The air sizzled between them. Anticipation rolled through her, and her lungs practically burned as she tried to drag in a breath. He stood up. His gaze traveled over her body slowly, appreciatively, and he reached out a trembling hand to touch her cheek.

"How did you know?" she asked.

"I didn't. I hoped and I prayed and you came to me."

The words ripped through her, causing a slow shudder. She pressed her open palm against the back of his hand. "I couldn't stay away. Maybe I never could. All I know right now is I don't care about the past or the future—I want you."

"Good, because I crave you, Chloe Lake. I'll try to go slow but I'm on the edge here."

She stepped into his embrace and thrust all ten fingers into his hair. "I don't need slow. I need us."

With a low growl, he took her mouth. The kiss was deep and soulful, with no polite re-introductions, just a slow, deep drag into pleasure and the bliss of how they fit together. His tongue dipped, tasted, plunged. He nipped at her lips, sipped like she was a sweet fruit, and stripped her naked with deliberate motions that made shivers break over her skin.

His hands roved everywhere, exploring, relearning, sliding over the curve of her hip, her tight nipples, the wet heat between her legs demanding more. He pushed his pants down and spread her out on the bed, where his mouth repeated every move of his fingers, and she was a twisted, writhing figure underneath him, begging for more.

She scraped her nails down his back, hooked her ankle around his, and arched up. His erection pressed against her inner thigh, and he gave a low laugh, tugging on her nipple, then licking with his tongue. "Not done with you yet. Not even close."

She gripped his pulsing length and squeezed. "We'll catch up later."

Owen groaned, growing bigger within her grip. "You don't fight fair."

"Never did."

"Neither do I." With one quick motion, he pushed her knees up, spread her legs wide, and dipped his mouth to her weeping center.

"Oh, God!"

He licked her, long and slow and sweet, murmuring sexy words as he pushed her straight to the edge. Curling two fingers, he pushed into her tight channel while his tongue played her like a beautiful instrument.

"Come, Chloe."

His lips wrapped around her throbbing clit, and he sucked hard.

She came with a scream ripped from the back of her throat. Pleasure broke over her, tearing her apart at the same time she flew to ecstatic heights. He murmured his approval, still tasting her, then quickly donned a condom and surged inside.

Blinking, her mind foggy from the orgasm, she stared into his hungry blue eyes, treasuring the familiar quirk to his lips. "You're so damn beautiful," he said, dropping a kiss on her swollen lips. "I've replayed this a million times in my head—the image of you and your orgasms, the way you give me everything you are. You're in my blood, babe. In my very soul." Buried deep, cock pulsing in demand, he uttered the words that brought her right to the brink, as she softened and opened to him, the final barrier laying in rubble around her heart. "I've never stopped loving you."

Then he began to move, each stroke claiming her all over again. She clung to his shoulders and arched upward to meet him stride for stride. Her clit scraped against his erection, her nipples rubbed against the rough hair of his chest, all while his mouth took hers in a wild, passionate kiss, his tongue repeating the motions of his driving hips, and then she exploded again, letting the orgasm wash over her and claim her in its grip.

He followed her over with a groan, his head thrown back as he released, and then he was gathering her in his arms, holding tight, and the past met the present and merged together, finally at peace.

Chapter Fourteen

He pressed slow, sleepy kisses over the sensitive curve of her neck. "Was it the dog?"

Chloe stretched her leg against him and let out a soft laugh against his damp chest. "No, but it helped."

"The cupcakes? My sexy charm? My riding skills?"

She studied him from under lowered lashes, savoring the delicious, musky scent of him. "It was the mix tape."

Owen stared at her in shock. "You're kidding. It's a playlist. Not a mix tape."

"Same thing. It touched me. Confirmed you remembered me."

His face softened, his large hand cupping her breast. "Babe, I couldn't forget you if I tried. I'm sorry if I ever made you believe that, but I'm here now." He paused, a frown creasing his brow. "How do you want to move forward? I don't know if I'd be able to handle pretending to be just friends when we're back in the office."

"I don't want that either. I'm done fighting, Owen." Though he'd already expressed he loved her, the words still got stuck in her throat. She wasn't ready yet, but she didn't want to go backwards. "We're dating exclusively. We're in a relationship. Let's start there."

He smiled with a gentleness that always touched her heart. "I can do that."

"Good. Now let's move on to more important things." She crawled on top of him, staring down at his naked body with pure hunger. He was all lean muscle and golden hair spread out for her enjoyment. His immediate erection sent a surge of power through her, and she lowered herself down, her hair brushing his chest, savoring his sucked-in breath. "Catching up."

She took her time with his body, tasting and touching, relishing every moan and needy arch. Kneeling between his legs, she took him deep in her mouth, sucking, tasting, her hands stroking his thighs until his control finally snapped, and he lifted her up, face frantic with need.

Chloe fit him with the condom and lowered herself down inch by slow inch until she'd taken him completely. The overwhelming feeling of being possessed completely washed over her, and she suddenly blinked back tears, moving on him and over him at a steady pace. He cupped her face, his thumb brushing back one of her tears, a guttural groan emitting from his throat.

But she didn't stop. She rode him and he captured every tear on her cheek, his gaze trapping hers, refusing to let go even as they both orgasmed together.

Then they fell into a tangle of limbs and slept.

* * * *

Two weeks later, Owen settled with Gus-Gus on the couch, pulling at the ragged chew rope in an endless game of tug of war. The chubby pup grit his sharp teeth with motivation, confident he'd be the winner against the rope, seemingly having no clue Owen was the one who controlled it.

The pup's teeth slid from the grip, and he tumbled onto his back, hind legs kicking as he tried to right himself like a turtle on its shell. Owen laughed and tickled his belly, and it dissolved into a complete love fest. The paw had completely healed and the pup was in full terror mode.

"I think we need to move, buddy," he said with a sigh. "This place isn't dog friendly, and I have a feeling you're going to be the first of many." Owen always knew he'd eventually need a place where he could have a few rescue pets comfortably. This had been a temporary place, but the fancy building was overly expensive, and he wanted simple. Of course, everything in New York was high-priced, and eventually he'd have to confront his salary and make a decision he didn't want.

The interview with Mario's firm had gone well. Too well. They'd offered him the job today. Besides being generously paid, he'd be involved in many high-profile cases. It seemed to be a no-brainer, even though it would be hard to leave the Animal Defense Fund, but something inside him made him hesitate and ask for time to think about it.

On paper, the job was perfect. He'd be able to afford more and offer more financial flexibility to Chloe, cementing a better future. Sure, it would be endless hours, and the clients were upper crust, with more money and connections than the not-for-profits population he regularly served.

But that shouldn't matter. He needed to grow up and do what was right. Be the type of man Chloe could count on for the future.

His mind chewed at his doubts like Gus-Gus with his rope. Maybe he needed to seriously consider taking this job along with some other changes. Since the farm, they'd fallen into an easy routine, spending some nights together, visiting rescues, taking care of Gus-Gus. She was allowing him into not just her heart, but her daily life, and that meant everything.

Sure, she still refused to say she loved him, but he sensed her emotions every time he took her in his arms. She just wasn't ready. Needed more time. More proof he wasn't going to rip away the foundation again. Making some smart decisions might help Chloe realize he was here to stay and serious about their future.

He now had too much to lose.

The phone buzzed, interrupting him.

Here.

He texted back. *Buzzing you in.*

"Mama's here, buddy. You'll have new fingers to chew on."

Gus-Gus bounced around, sensing a new arriver, and Owen laughed as he opened the door.

"How's my baby?" she cooed, running right past Owen to the furball. Gus-Gus jumped around her, barking and rolling around in a fit of ecstasy.

Owen raised both hands in the air. "What about me?"

She blew him an air kiss from the floor, hugging and cuddling the puppy. "How's my baby?" she asked him teasingly.

"Cute." He closed the door and dropped beside her, claiming his kiss while Gus-Gus tried to climb between them with his wriggly body. "How was the meeting?"

"Good, I think I made an impression on the board to consider Advocates for Animals for part of their holiday funding program. Did you hear back from the court on your motion?"

"The trial is going forth—the judge denied their extension."

Her gaze grew hard. "Good. Thank goodness, they're not letting the

Spagarellis play their games. Sometimes I really hate money. They get themselves some fancy-ass lawyers and drag us endlessly through motions, burying us in paperwork. I'm so happy we work for organizations that help people who really need it."

He winced. Not the best segue way into his announcement of a new position, but he'd talk it through with her. "Chloe, I wanted to talk to you about—"

Her phone blared and she shot him an apologetic look. "I'm so sorry, it's Vivian, I just need to take this."

He nodded, playing with Gus-Gus while she chatted. Then her face suddenly went pale and her voice hissed over the phone. "He did what?"

Owen tilted his head, watching her.

"I can't believe it—can he do that? Isn't it illegal to promise funds and then go back on your word? Didn't we have the paperwork filed and approved?"

He waited while she went back and forth, obviously upset, then finally clicked off. "What happened?" he asked.

"Drew pulled the funds from our organization," she said bitterly. "Said the Foundation changed their minds after reviewing our application and decided on another rescue organization."

"Son of a bitch," he muttered. "I'm so sorry, Chloe. How bad will it affect you?"

"Bad. Vivian is in battle mode, trying to see if we can rally some donors. We'd earmarked the funds for a few legal cases we wanted to take on, along with purchasing those new kennels for some of our partners. Damnit, how could he do this to me?"

"He wants to hurt you because you didn't choose him," Owen said simply. "He never realized you could never love someone who cares more about himself than others."

She fisted her hands and paced. Gus-Gus bounded over and followed in her footsteps. "I wish there was something I could do, but I have no networking ability with that board. Drew was the one who's been promising the funds for the last few months."

"We'll figure something out. Maybe I can rally some troops to take on some pro-bono cases for you. We'll meet with Vivian tomorrow and create a plan."

She crossed over and hugged him, allowing comfort. He buried his face in her hair, breathing deep, and savored her. "Thanks for having my back."

"Every time, babe."

He kissed her, nipping at her lower lip, dipping his tongue in her sweet, wet heat and immediately went hard. He craved scooping her up and carrying her into bed, but he needed to have the dialogue with her now. "I have news to share."

"Oh, I like news," she murmured, dropping kisses on his jawline. "Tell me."

"I got a new job offer. With Dooney and Finklestein Legal Associates."

She stilled, then slowly drew back. A frown marred her brow. "What do you mean? I never knew you were interested in leaving the Animal Defense Fund."

"I wasn't. But I met Mario at the courthouse and they've been looking for a new associate. I'd be strictly animal law, of course, and the pay is double what I'm making. They have a good reputation."

"Yes, they do. I don't have an issue with that. I'm just surprised. Don't they cater to the country club crowd?"

Frustration shot through him. "Rich people have a great deal of influence on changes in law."

"I know. But I thought one of the things you were most passionate about is protecting and defending the ones who can't pay. The ones who can't afford the fancy-ass lawyers."

His jaw clenched. He didn't like the uneasy feelings her words brought up, or the challenge suddenly gleaming in her eyes. He spoke calmly. "I do, but I also need to be practical. This is a steady job where I can pick my clients, make money, and still make a difference. You know how not-for-profits run—one day the budget is cut and you're out of a job."

"Sure, but that's another reason we're so needed. There's fewer and fewer people fighting for them. Look at the Spagarelli case. If it wasn't for you and the Defense Fund pursuing, that couple would have never paid for their crime. Even worse, they'd keep doing it over and over again, because no one stops them."

He blew out a breath. "I haven't even tried the case yet, Chloe. I may not win."

She tilted her head and studied him. "You already won, because you haven't given up. If you lose this one, we'll be keeping a close eye on them, and be ready to pounce. We'll get justice eventually."

He stared at her stubborn conviction, the gleam of determination in her blue eyes, the fierce energy that radiated from her figure, so like her father. God, she was such a warrior, refusing to surrender, but would living this life with him one day cause burnout? Would she crave stability and security more than the fight for justice?

"Owen, tell me what's going on." She took his hand and pressed it against her heart. "You can tell me anything."

He hesitated, wanting to spill his fears to the woman he trusted more than anyone.

Instead, he shot her a smile and shook his head. "Nothing, babe. Let me think a bit and we can talk more later. For now, I think we need to deal with the process of getting Gus-Gus to bed. Can you help me?"

The disappointment in her gaze hurt more than he anticipated. As if she sensed he hid something important from her. But she forced her own smile. "Sure."

After they settled Gus-Gus, he made love to her, wringing out her orgasms, claiming her with a fierce hunger and possession that almost broke him apart. And after, he whispered the only thing he could make sure he gave her.

"I love you."

Once again, she held him close but didn't answer.

Chapter Fifteen

Chloe squeezed her pink stress ball and wondered what was haunting Owen.

They'd been steadily building a new foundation between them separate from the past. For the first time, she sensed an even stronger connection with the people they'd grown into and was beginning to understand more about why he'd needed to leave.

She liked being with a man who walked his own path. Watching him in his element, pursuing his own passions on his own terms, was a heady aphrodisiac. He'd changed in all ways except one.

His heart. It was still loving, kind, and open.

And it was still hers.

She sighed and glanced over at his empty desk. She hadn't given him the words yet, and she wasn't sure why. She knew she loved him, but when she opened her mouth, a strange fear struck her mute. He never pushed, but there was an underlying tension beginning to grow between them. And when he shared the possibility of taking the law firm job, she couldn't help being shocked. He'd always told her how happy he was with his job and the transfer; he bubbled over with ideas to recruit more lawyers for not-for-profit and compose new intern programs.

Transferring to a private firm where he'd be forced to prosecute a few handpicked cases from rich clients stole away his freedom. When she looked into his eyes, it was clear he had doubts and didn't want to take it. Why did he keep talking about money? Neither of them had ever focused on money as a goal. Had something suddenly changed she couldn't figure out?

Chloe grabbed her phone and dialed.

"Hi, sweetheart. You got me for five minutes before my next meeting. I'm walking there now."

"Oh, it's nothing, Dad. Just wanted to say hello."

She heard a whooshing sound, then his voice low in the phone. "Bull. I can hear from your tone, you never call me in the middle of the day to just say hi. Is it Owen?"

She laughed, rubbing her temple. "Yes, but not how you think it is. We're still deliriously happy. It's just, something weird is going on with him and I thought I'd get your perspective."

"Shoot."

She explained the job offer, Owen's reaction, and the mention of money. "He kept looking at me funny and repeating that the money was good, and the job was secure."

"Nothing wrong with that. Maybe he's trying to show you he's serious about your relationship. That he can take care of you for the future."

She practically gagged, then heard a loud yell from Alyssa. "Ouch, okay, sorry. Chloe? Alyssa said that was egotistical and chauvinistic and that you need no one to take care of yourself but you."

A smile curved her lips. "Good. She's right."

"I know. But maybe Owen is stuck on a battle plan. You know instead of trying to woo you to date him, he's trying to woo you to settle down and trust him in a committed relationship."

She blew out a breath. "Dad, you're not making sense to me."

"Okay, let's try again. See, men get caught up with this old-fashioned ideal of being worthy of the women we love. Maybe Owen is just trying to prove he's a good risk for your heart. That he won't leave you again. Money, to many, equals security. Maturity. Happiness. You may want to ask him if he wants to take this job for you."

Her jaw dropped as the sudden realization slammed through her. "How do I get him to admit it?"

A door slammed. A few mutters drifted in the air. "Not sure. Maybe take a risk. Give him something you're afraid of too, and then you'll be even. You really love him, don't you?"

Her voice softened. "Yeah, I really love him."

"Good. I found out Drew is an asshole. Heard he pulled your funds from his Foundation."

"How do you know that?"

"I'm the governor. I try to know everything in my state, especially when it affects your organization. You'll be receiving a call from Carlos—he worked with Harper at the Thoroughbred Retirement Foundation. He's putting your name in for a brand-new grant. Sorry, sweetheart, gotta go. Good luck—call me tonight."

The phone clicked.

God, she loved her father. She was so lucky to have him in her life.

Chloe laid the phone carefully on her desk. Suddenly everything began to make sense. The pressure from their past combined with Jonathan's demands for him to be worthy of her, of Drew's questioning, of his grandfather's legacy—too many voices had gotten into his head in his quest for perfection.

She needed to show him they'd never be perfect. That he didn't have to be worthy of her.

They needed to be worthy of each other.

It was time to take the risk.

* * * *

When Owen walked into his apartment, he thought there was a power outage.

He blinked in the darkness, then focused on the endless flicker of candlelight that seemed to burst from every corner. Gus-Gus bounded over in a frenzy, and Owen scooped him up, laughing as he wriggled against him in pure delight. "Hey, buddy, do you know what's going on?"

"I'm cooking us dinner."

He moved farther into the room and saw her. It took a few minutes for his big brain to kick in, because his little one had taken over.

Chloe stood in his kitchen dressed in a frilly black apron.

And nothing else.

He tried to speak, found he had no spit, and tried again. "Aren't those pizza boxes?"

She tossed him a cheeky grin, her long, naked legs on full display. Full breasts strained against the black apron, ready to pop out any moment. He prayed really hard for her to turn around. "Yes, but I'm reheating them in the oven since you're late."

"Sorry, got stuck at court. Umm, have I told you lately you're the hottest woman on the planet?"

"No, but I like that."

She turned and he almost fell to his knees. Dear God, her ass was pure, curvy perfection. She swiveled back around way too soon. "Would you like to go to the bedroom first? Or after pizza?"

He stared at her, blinking.

"Owen?"

"Oh, now, please."

"First, let's talk. Sit and drink your beer."

"Okay." He had no brain waves left anyway; they all had left his body with one glance at her naked body. "What do you want to talk about? Can it be fast?"

She gave a low laugh and handed him the beer. He gulped greedily, trying to saturate his parched throat, and wondered if he'd fallen asleep in the courthouse and this was just a dream. Hell, if it was, he didn't want to wake up.

"I want to ask you a few questions. You just tell me the truth. Deal?"

"Deal."

"Do you really want that job at Mario's firm?"

He jerked. She'd managed to surprise him. All his snappy answers and defenses had seemed to disappear along with his brain, so he just talked. "I like the benefits, and the pay, and the idea of it. But no, I really don't want the job."

She gave a sigh of relief. "Thank you for telling me the truth. Why were you considering it then? Was it because of me?"

He didn't answer. Something told him not to say anything, but he was staring at her left breast, and the nipple was hard and almost falling out of the lace and he got confused. "A little."

"Why?" she demanded. "I need to know why you'd think I wanted you to have that job."

"I don't want to mess up again, babe," he finally said. "I can't lose you, and I'm afraid you may eventually get frustrated with this type of living. You deserve a fat apartment, and designer clothes, and five-star restaurants on a regular basis. You deserve to stay home without struggle if we decide to have a baby one day. You deserve everything."

The release of his secret fears gave him a rush of lightness. He practically slumped in the chair with shame and relief, but then suddenly, she was sitting on his lap. Her warm, curvy body wrapped around him and she cupped his cheeks, forcing him to look at her. "Look around you right now."

"I can't, you're holding my face."

"Okay, you don't need to look. Want to know my dream? To get up every day and have a job that makes a difference. To be passionate about what I do and have my goal worthy."

"You already have that."

"Exactly. That was the first portion. The second is you. Having the man I love, fighting side by side for the same cause, loving me for who I am without ever asking me to change."

"You have that, too."

She smiled, and her scent filled his nostrils and he fell headfirst into ocean blue eyes that captured his very soul. "Exactly. I want dogs."

"You have Gus-Gus and we can get more."

"Yes. I think that covers it all. Money means nothing to me, Owen. I want us to love each other and be true to who we are—that's what I truly need."

"Then this was all in my head? You think I'll always be enough?"

She made a fierce sound and then she was kissing him, her tongue plunging between his lips to make her own claim, and he gave her all of it, holding her tight against him. "You're the man I love, Owen Salt. I love you with everything I am. The moment we danced that first time, my heart was never truly mine. It was just waiting for you."

The words ripped him open and made him whole. He lifted her up and carried her into the bedroom, stumbling around Gus-Gus as he wove in between him, desperate to follow. He lay her on the bed, taking in her spectacular naked glory, and deposited the puppy outside the door.

"The things I'm going to do to you are too dirty for him to see," he said with a low growl.

"Do them."

And he did.

Epilogue

Chloe stepped back from the crowd, squinting in the flashing bulbs that exploded around her. A reporter jammed a mic at her, rattling off question after question as she walked down the steps of the courthouse and took her place by his side.

Owen was already speaking. "…proud of the verdict in a clear case of animal abuse and neglect. Hopefully, this will set a precedent for many other cases where we need to protect the helpless and be their voice."

"Chloe, are you getting married?"

"Chloe—will you be working with Mr. Salt on further abuse cases?"

"Chloe—what designer will you be wearing for the Met Gala?"

Owen looked down at her and grinned, his hand firmly in hers. She gave her public dazzling smile she'd learned years ago. "One day; yes; and a vintage dress I scored at the Second Chance thrift shop. Now if you'll excuse me, I need to get back to fighting for the animals, but I'm sure Mr. Salt will be happy to answer more questions."

With a saucy wink, she squeezed Owen's hand and made her exit, eventually spilling into the sidewalk crowd and losing herself in the city she loved and her father would always fight for.

It was nice for Owen to be in the spotlight for a change, and his work had been receiving a large amount of press, instituting a new wave for not-for-profit volunteers, interns, and employees. They had big plans, but today was special. It was the first stop in a long journey that would always end up with the man she loved.

Owen Salt.

She walked into the jewelry store where the portly man behind the counter rushed over to greet her. "May I help you?"

"I'm Chloe Lake, I have an appointment to look at rings."

His face lit up. "Yes! Come this way, Ms. Lake, I have the most amazing ones to show you. Can I just tell you it's so refreshing to see the number of women who are now proposing? About time the world realized there's no reason to wait when you finally found the one."

Chloe smiled, her insides fluttering with excitement. "Thank you, I agree."

She'd never been one to wait on a happy ever after.

She was her father's daughter. And she'd found her prince years ago, her first love, her forever love.

Tonight, she'd ask Owen to marry her and he'd say yes.

She couldn't wait.

Second chances were sometimes the sweetest of all.

The End

* * * *

Also from 1001 Dark Nights and Jennifer Probst, discover Something Just Like This, The Marriage Arrangement, Somehow, Some Way and Searching for Mine.

Author's Note

Animal rescue is a passion of mine. When I was writing about the Bishop farm, I knew my secondary characters were going to be just as important as my primary –with big personalities, conflicts, and their own healing journey. I loved writing about Phoenix, the abused rescue horse; Captain Hoof, his blind goat companion, and of course, Hei-Hei, my fabulous, cranky Polish chicken.

The moment Chloe showed up as an angry nineteen-year-old girl in *The Start of Something Good*, I knew she'd make a difference in the world of animal rescue. Watching Owen follow the same path was a sign they were always meant to be together. I'm grateful you followed me on this journey to watch our final couple find their happy ever after.

I've noted some organizations in this book that I personally donate time and money to. Sidewalk Angels supports pet rescue and other causes. Pets Alive has inspired many of my animal characters and does amazing work. I adopted my own two rescue dogs at Barking Back Rescue. I encourage you to donate to these or any local organizations who make a difference for our furry creatures.

I also want to thank Neil Abramson, an amazing writer who penned *Unsaid* and *Just Life*. Thanks for taking the time to answer my questions and provide so much valuable information.

Finally, thanks to Liz Berry, MJ Rose, and Jillian Stein for allowing me to write in the 1001 Dark Nights world – it's an honor!

www.petsalive.com
https://www.sidewalkangelsfoundation.org/
https://www.barkingback.org/

Sign up for the 1001 Dark Nights Newsletter
and be entered to win a Tiffany Key necklace.

There's a contest every month!

Go to www.1001DarkNights.com to subscribe.

As a bonus, all subscribers can download
FIVE FREE exclusive books!

Discover 1001 Dark Nights Collection Seven

Visit www.1001DarkNights.com for more information.

THE BISHOP by Skye Warren
A Tanglewood Novella

TAKEN WITH YOU by Carrie Ann Ryan
A Fractured Connections Novella

DRAGON LOST by Donna Grant
A Dark Kings Novella

SEXY LOVE by Carly Phillips
A Sexy Series Novella

PROVOKE by Rachel Van Dyken
A Seaside Pictures Novella

RAFE by Sawyer Bennett
An Arizona Vengeance Novella

THE NAUGHTY PRINCESS by Claire Contreras
A Sexy Royals Novella

THE GRAVEYARD SHIFT by Darynda Jones
A Charley Davidson Novella

CHARMED by Lexi Blake
A Masters and Mercenaries Novella

SACRIFICE OF DARKNESS by Alexandra Ivy
A Guardians of Eternity Novella

THE QUEEN by Jen Armentrout
A Wicked Novella

BEGIN AGAIN by Jennifer Probst
A Stay Novella

VIXEN by Rebecca Zanetti
A Dark Protectors/Rebels Novella

SLASH by Laurelin Paige
A Slay Series Novella

THE DEAD HEAT OF SUMMER by Heather Graham
A Krewe of Hunters Novella

WILD FIRE by Kristen Ashley
A Chaos Novella

MORE THAN PROTECT YOU by Shayla Black
A More Than Words Novella

LOVE SONG by Kylie Scott
A Stage Dive Novella

CHERISH ME by J. Kenner
A Stark Ever After Novella

SHINE WITH ME by Kristen Proby
A With Me in Seattle Novella

And new from Blue Box Press:

TEASE ME by J. Kenner
A Stark International Novel

FROM BLOOD AND ASH by Jennifer L. Armentrout
A Blood and Ash Novel

QUEEN MOVE by Kennedy Ryan

THE BUTTERFLY ROOM by Lucinda Riley

A KINGDOM OF FLESH AND FIRE by Jennifer L. Armentrout
A Blood and Ash Novel

Discover More Jennifer Probst

Something Just Like This: A Stay Novella

Jonathan Lake is the beloved NYC mayor who's making a run for governor. His widowed status and close relationship with his daughter casts him as the darling of the press, and the candidate to beat, but behind the flash of the cameras, things are spinning out of control. It all has to do with his strait laced, ruthlessly organized assistant. Her skills and reserved demeanor are perfect to run his campaign, but her brilliant brain has become a temptation he's been fighting for too long. Can he convince her to take a chance on a long-term campaign for love or will his efforts end up in scandal?

Alyssa Block has admired the NYC mayor for a long time, but her secret crush is kept ruthlessly buried under a mountain of work. Besides, she's not his type, and office scandals are not in her job description. But when they retreat to an upstate horse farm for a secluded weekend, the spark between them catches flame, and Jonathan sets those stinging blue eyes on winning her. Can she convince him to focus on the upcoming election, or will she succumb to the sweet promise of a different future?

* * * *

The Marriage Arrangement: A Marriage to a Billionaire Novella

She had run from her demons…

Caterina Victoria Windsor fled her family winery after a humiliating broken engagement, and spent the past year in Italy rebuilding her world. But when Ripley Savage shows up with a plan to bring her back home, and an outrageous demand for her to marry him, she has no choice but to return to face her past. But when simple attraction begins to run deeper, Cat has to decide if she's strong enough to trust again…and strong enough to stay…

He vowed to bring her back home to be his wife…

Rip Savage saved Windsor Winery, but the only way to make it truly his is to marry into the family. He's not about to walk away from the only thing he's ever wanted, even if he has to tame the spoiled brat who left her legacy and her father behind without a care. When he convinces her to agree to a marriage arrangement and return home, he never counted on the fierce sexual attraction between them to grow into something more. But when deeper emotions emerge, Rip has to fight for something he wants even more than Windsor Winery: his future wife.

* * * *

Somehow, Some Way: A Billionaire Builders Novella

Bolivar Randy Heart (aka Brady) knows exactly what he wants next in life: the perfect wife. Raised in a strict traditional family household, he seeks a woman who is sweet, conservative, and eager to settle down. With his well-known protective and dominant streak, he needs a woman to offer him balance in a world where he relishes control.

Too bad the newly hired, gorgeous rehab addict is blasting through all his preconceptions and wrecking his ideals…one nail at a time…

Charlotte Grayson knows who she is and refuses to apologize. Growing up poor made her appreciate the simple things in life, and her new job at Pierce Brothers Construction is perfect to help her carve out a career in renovating houses. When an opportunity to transform a dilapidated house in a dangerous neighborhood pops up, she goes in full throttle. Unfortunately, she's forced to work with the firm's sexy architect who's driving her crazy with his archaic views on women.

Too bad he's beginning to tempt her to take a chance on more than just work…one stroke at a time…

Somehow, some way, they need to work together to renovate a house without killing each other…or surrendering to the white-hot chemistry knocking at the front door.

* * * *

Searching for Mine: A Searching For Novella

The Ultimate Anti-Hero Meets His Match…

Connor Dunkle knows what he wants in a woman, and it's the three B's. Beauty. Body. Boobs. Other women need not apply. With his good looks and easygoing charm, he's used to getting what he wants—and who. Until he comes face to face with the one woman who's slowly making his life hell...and enjoying every moment...

Ella Blake is a single mom and a professor at the local Verily College who's climbed up the ranks the hard way. Her ten-year-old son is a constant challenge, and her students are driving her crazy—namely Connor Dunkle, who's failing her class and trying to charm his way into a better grade. Fuming at his chauvinistic tendencies, Ella teaches him the ultimate lesson by giving him a *special* project to help his grade. When sparks fly, neither of them are ready to face their true feelings, but will love teach them the ultimate lesson of all?

Something Just Like This
By Jennifer Probst
A Stay Novella

From *New York Times* and *USA Today* bestselling author Jennifer Probst comes a new story in her Stay series.

Jonathan Lake is the beloved NYC mayor who's making a run for governor. His widowed status and close relationship with his daughter casts him as the darling of the press, and the candidate to beat, but behind the flash of the cameras, things are spinning out of control. It all has to do with his strait laced, ruthlessly organized assistant. Her skills and reserved demeanor are perfect to run his campaign, but her brilliant brain has become a temptation he's been fighting for too long. Can he convince her to take a chance on a long-term campaign for love or will his efforts end up in scandal?

Alyssa Block has admired the NYC mayor for a long time, but her secret crush is kept ruthlessly buried under a mountain of work. Besides, she's not his type, and office scandals are not in her job description. But when they retreat to an upstate horse farm for a secluded weekend, the spark between them catches flame, and Jonathan sets those stinging blue-eyes on winning her. Can she convince him to focus on the upcoming election, or will she succumb to the sweet promise of a different future?

* * * *

Chapter One

"I want you to run for governor."
Jonathan Lake stared down at his clasped hands as the fateful words echoed in his head. Less than an hour ago, he'd had a closed-door meeting with the current governor, who informed him he was not seeking re-election. It'd be a shock to the party, but they'd already focused in on the candidate they believed had a solid shot at winning.

Him.

Oh, the shit was about to hit the proverbial fan. Once the story got out, it'd be a shark-feeding frenzy with him smack in the middle of the red waters. Did he really want this? He'd only been mayor for one term and was just beginning to settle into the job. New York City was a dirty bastard, but he loved every grimy, fierce, beautiful inch of it, from the concrete to the skyscrapers. Was he even ready to move on and take on the entire state?

His late wife's voice whispered in his ear, even after all these years.

This is what you were meant for.

Pushing his fingers through his hair, he got up from his chair and began to pace his office. Thoughts whirled in his head, making him feel as if he'd overindulged in martinis at lunch. So much to think about. He'd call his daughter Chloe and get her feedback. And, of course, Mia, who handled his PR. He'd tell Bob, his campaign manager, in the morning. The former marine would be working his ass off nonstop for the next year—might as well give him one last evening free. But there was one woman on his mind. One who not only ran his schedule but also his entire life. The woman he trusted as fiercely as he did Chloe and Mia.

He strode over to the desk and hit the button. "Can you come in here, please?"

The clipped, cool voice echoed in the air. "Of course."

He counted down the eight seconds it always took her to move from her desk to his office, and the door opened on cue. She entered with the smooth, assured stride he'd memorized and slid into her chair opposite his desk, her tablet held between tapered fingers with short, naked nails. She wore her usual black pantsuit and low-heeled black pumps. Once he'd joked if she had seven identical pantsuits in her closet for each day of the week.

She'd said they were all black, but not identical because they were different designers and fabric, and she kept an eighth outfit available for emergencies. She didn't understand jokes very well. Her sense of humor was Spock-like, and it had taken him a while to get used to it.

He stared at the nape of her neck, exposed from the ruthless topknot she kept her ash-blond hair tied in, her gaze trained on the screen in front of her. He knew the gaze well. Big, brown eyes hidden behind smart, tortoiseshell-framed glasses. Razor-focused. Ruthlessly composed. Sharply intelligent. A bit distant.

And endlessly fascinating.

"No notes," he clipped out, resuming his pacing. "I need to discuss something with you."

"He wants you to run for governor."

He jerked, then wondered why he was surprised. Her IQ wasn't just off the charts on paper, but she could also read people. The combination made her the best damn right-hand person he'd ever employed in his life. It also made her completely irreplaceable—and she knew it.

"Yes. He's decided not to run for re-election and thinks I can win."

She never tried to turn her head to gaze at him, allowing him to pace his office like the cage it sometimes was. Her aura seeped a calmness that already soothed the wild chatter in his mind. She was almost witchlike in her ability to give him whatever he needed. Maybe that was why he'd begun thinking of her as much more than his assistant and advisor.

Or maybe he was finally starting to break under his long-imposed years of celibacy.

"You can win," she said. "Statistically, you're the best choice. Your approval ratings are top-rated. You're coming off a victory of reducing the amount of homelessness in the city, and your political views are balanced so the liberals and conservatives will both be satisfied. You're a dream candidate, Mr. Mayor, and our governor has never been stupid. He endorses you, steps out of the spotlight, and gives you a clear path to victory."

"Stop calling me that," he barked, irritation prickling his skin. "We're alone. I told you this before."

She inclined her head with grace. "Sorry, Jonathan."

His name on her tongue calmed the beast. He dropped into his leather chair and drummed his fingers on the table, staring at her. She stared back, unblinking, waiting patiently for whatever he wanted to throw at her.

Damnit. He'd hired her because she knew her shit, came highly recommended, and they'd never want to sleep with each other. His last hire had been a mistake, one who ended up crushing on him and failing at her job. His long-term assistant had finally succumbed to retirement, and he'd been floundering at the loss. The moment Alyssa Block had walked into his office with her cool eyes and clipped speech, he'd known they weren't each other's types. He preferred fiery, opinionated, passionate women like his beloved late wife. A partner who challenged him mentally and physically. It was also obvious that Alyssa didn't give a crap about flirting with him or being physical—she just wanted to do her job the best she could.

That had been over two years ago, and they'd been inseparable ever since. In a good way.

He'd learned early on that mixing business with personal

relationships meant disaster—any politician who wanted a career knew the rules to follow. History proved itself over and over. Men who couldn't keep their pants zipped made for crappy leaders. He didn't get involved in opinions, whether it was right or wrong for his personal life to be scrutinized and judged. Jonathan only dealt with the facts, and if he couldn't change them or tweak them, acceptance was the best route.

He never thought it'd be a problem. Until lately.

Because, lately, he'd been thinking about Alyssa in many more ways than as his assistant. And it was wrecking the entire orderly world that she so competently managed for him.

About Jennifer Probst

Jennifer Probst wrote her first book at twelve years old. She bound it in a folder, read it to her classmates, and hasn't stopped writing since. She holds a masters in English Literature and lives in the beautiful Hudson Valley in upstate New York. Her family keeps her active, stressed, joyous, and sad her house will never be truly clean. Her passions include horse racing, Scrabble, rescue dogs, Italian food, and wine—not necessarily in that order.

She is the *New York Times*, *USA Today*, and *Wall Street Journal* bestselling author of sexy and erotic contemporary romance. She was thrilled her book, *The Marriage Bargain*, spent 26 weeks on the *New York Times*. Her work has been translated in over a dozen countries, sold over a million copies, and was dubbed a "romance phenom" by Kirkus Reviews. She is also a proud three-time RITA finalist.

She loves hearing from readers. Visit her website for updates on new releases and her street team at www.jenniferprobst.com.

Discover 1001 Dark Nights

Visit www.1001DarkNights.com for more information.

COLLECTION THREE
HIDDEN INK by Carrie Ann Ryan
BLOOD ON THE BAYOU by Heather Graham
SEARCHING FOR MINE by Jennifer Probst
DANCE OF DESIRE by Christopher Rice
ROUGH RHYTHM by Tessa Bailey
DEVOTED by Lexi Blake
Z by Larissa Ione
FALLING UNDER YOU by Laurelin Paige
EASY FOR KEEPS by Kristen Proby
UNCHAINED by Elisabeth Naughton
HARD TO SERVE by Laura Kaye
DRAGON FEVER by Donna Grant
KAYDEN/SIMON by Alexandra Ivy/Laura Wright
STRUNG UP by Lorelei James
MIDNIGHT UNTAMED by Lara Adrian
TRICKED by Rebecca Zanetti
DIRTY WICKED by Shayla Black
THE ONLY ONE by Lauren Blakely
SWEET SURRENDER by Liliana Hart

COLLECTION FOUR
ROCK CHICK REAWAKENING by Kristen Ashley
ADORING INK by Carrie Ann Ryan
SWEET RIVALRY by K. Bromberg
SHADE'S LADY by Joanna Wylde
RAZR by Larissa Ione
ARRANGED by Lexi Blake
TANGLED by Rebecca Zanetti
HOLD ME by J. Kenner
SOMEHOW, SOME WAY by Jennifer Probst
TOO CLOSE TO CALL by Tessa Bailey
HUNTED by Elisabeth Naughton
EYES ON YOU by Laura Kaye
BLADE by Alexandra Ivy/Laura Wright
DRAGON BURN by Donna Grant
TRIPPED OUT by Lorelei James
STUD FINDER by Lauren Blakely
MIDNIGHT UNLEASHED by Lara Adrian

HALLOW BE THE HAUNT by Heather Graham
DIRTY FILTHY FIX by Laurelin Paige
THE BED MATE by Kendall Ryan
NIGHT GAMES by CD Reiss
NO RESERVATIONS by Kristen Proby
DAWN OF SURRENDER by Liliana Hart

COLLECTION FIVE
BLAZE ERUPTING by Rebecca Zanetti
ROUGH RIDE by Kristen Ashley
HAWKYN by Larissa Ione
RIDE DIRTY by Laura Kaye
ROME'S CHANCE by Joanna Wylde
THE MARRIAGE ARRANGEMENT by Jennifer Probst
SURRENDER by Elisabeth Naughton
INKED NIGHTS by Carrie Ann Ryan
ENVY by Rachel Van Dyken
PROTECTED by Lexi Blake
THE PRINCE by Jennifer L. Armentrout
PLEASE ME by J. Kenner
WOUND TIGHT by Lorelei James
STRONG by Kylie Scott
DRAGON NIGHT by Donna Grant
TEMPTING BROOKE by Kristen Proby
HAUNTED BE THE HOLIDAYS by Heather Graham
CONTROL by K. Bromberg
HUNKY HEARTBREAKER by Kendall Ryan
THE DARKEST CAPTIVE by Gena Showalter

COLLECTION SIX
DRAGON CLAIMED by Donna Grant
ASHES TO INK by Carrie Ann Ryan
ENSNARED by Elisabeth Naughton
EVERMORE by Corinne Michaels
VENGEANCE by Rebecca Zanetti
ELI'S TRIUMPH by Joanna Wylde
CIPHER by Larissa Ione
RESCUING MACIE by Susan Stoker
ENCHANTED by Lexi Blake

TAKE THE BRIDE by Carly Phillips
INDULGE ME by J. Kenner
THE KING by Jennifer L. Armentrout
QUIET MAN by Kristen Ashley
ABANDON by Rachel Van Dyken
THE OPEN DOOR by Laurelin Paige
CLOSER by Kylie Scott
SOMETHING JUST LIKE THIS by Jennifer Probst
BLOOD NIGHT by Heather Graham
TWIST OF FATE by Jill Shalvis
MORE THAN PLEASURE YOU by Shayla Black
WONDER WITH ME by Kristen Proby
THE DARKEST ASSASSIN by Gena Showalter

Discover Blue Box Press

TAME ME by J. Kenner
TEMPT ME by J. Kenner
DAMIEN by J. Kenner
TEASE ME by J. Kenner
REAPER by Larissa Ione
THE SURRENDER GATE by Christopher Rice
SERVICING THE TARGET by Cherise Sinclair
THE LAKE OF LEARNING by Steve Berry and MJ Rose
THE MUSEUM OF MYSTERIES by Steve Berry and MJ Rose

On Behalf of 1001 Dark Nights,

Liz Berry, M.J. Rose, and Jillian Stein would like to thank ~

Steve Berry
Doug Scofield
Benjamin Stein
Kim Guidroz
Social Butterfly PR
Asha Hossain
Chris Graham
Chelle Olson
Kasi Alexander
Jessica Johns
Dylan Stockton
Richard Blake
and Simon Lipskar

Made in the USA
Monee, IL
06 August 2020